TALES FROM
THE BUCCANEER
LODGE

Frank Leaman

BOULDER
BOOKS

Library and Archives Canada Cataloguing in Publication

Title: Tales from the Buccaneer Lodge / Frank Leaman.
Names: Leaman, Frank Crowell, author.
Identifiers: Canadiana 20210111240 | ISBN 9781989417102 (softcover)
Subjects: LCSH: Leaman, Frank Crowell—Anecdotes. | LCSH: Fishing lodges—Nova Scotia—Anecdotes. |
  LCSH: Boats and boating—Nova Scotia—Anecdotes. | LCSH: Aquatic sports—Nova Scotia—Anecdotes. |
  LCSH: Nova Scotia—History—Anecdotes. | LCSH: Nova Scotia—Biography—Anecdotes. | LCGFT: Anecdotes.
Classification: LCC SH572.N69 L43 2021 | DDC 799.109716—dc23 © 2021
Frank Leaman

Published by Boulder Books
Portugal Cove-St. Philip's, Newfoundland and Labrador
www.boulderbooks.ca

Design and layout: Tanya Montini
Editor: Stephanie Porter
Copy editor: Iona Bulgin

Printed in Canada

Excerpts from this publication may be reproduced under licence from
Access Copyright, or with the express written permission of Boulder Books Ltd.,
or as permitted by law. All rights are otherwise reserved and no part
of this publications may be reproduced, stored in a retrieval system,
or transmitted in any form or by any means, electronic, mechanical,
photocopying, scanning, recording, or otherwise,
except as specifically authorized.

We acknowledge the financial support of the Government of
Newfoundland and Labrador through the Department of Tourism,
Culture, Industry and Innovation.

Table of Contents

Introduction 5

CHAPTER 1
The Buccaneer Lodge and the *Buccaneer Lady* 15

CHAPTER 2
Tancook Island and the Island of Mystery 53

CHAPTER 3
Life around the Dartmouth Pier. 69

Chapter 4
The Early Days of Cable Television
in Rural Nova Scotia. 99

CHAPTER 5
Surplus Goods 115

CHAPTER 6
Moving On 137

Epilogue 145

About the Author 151

Introduction

These stories are of ships, people, and events that happened around me. I've tried my best to recount them as I remember them, but my memory can't always be trusted to tell the absolute truth.

My writing friends call me the Maud Lewis of writers because I write the way I talk. I'm not as literary as some of the others in my writing group in Dartmouth, Nova Scotia, where I live. They think my stories are like the folk artist's paintings, but instead of pictures of brightly coloured flowers, birds, and butterflies, I write simple stories of old ships, the characters who travelled on them, and the unpredictable life of a seaside innkeeper.

"You must be 150 years old because of all you have

Frank Leaman

done," they tell me. I'm not, but some days I feel I could be. I still have a couple of decades to go before I reach the 100-year milestone.

My life has revolved around Halifax harbour, Mahone Bay, and my father, Frank Manual Leaman. We ran seven businesses together and that meant a lot of juggling. Often, I started my day in Dartmouth, across the harbour from Halifax, and ended it an hour's drive away in the village of Chester on Nova Scotia's South Shore.

My father was a larger-than-life figure. He was a visionary. In the North End of Dartmouth, where he and I were both born, there is a street called Leaman Drive. We built that street. It almost broke us, but we built it. It was around 1953 or 1954 when my father bought about 225 acres of land in the area from the prominent Stairs family, made up of merchants and shippers. Believing that the area was going to grow, my father envisioned turning the land, home to Big Albro Lake and Little Albro Lake, into subdivisions. By selling two of these lots of land to a developer he got enough money to buy a hunting and fishing lodge in Chester in the late 1950s and enter the

Tales From the Buccaneer Lodge

province's adventure tourism business.

It was a bright, sunny day at the courthouse in Chester when the sheriff's hammer came down on the final bid that made my father the new owner of Owl's Head Lodge and Tuna Camps in East Chester. We later changed the name to the Buccaneer Motel and Cottages, or as we liked to call it, the Buccaneer Lodge.

The courthouse was full. Lots of people wanted the lodge and 11 acres of seaside waterfront property. My father had money, so he got it. We don't have any records of exactly how much the sale was for, but it was expensive for the time.

That day at the courtroom my father wore a suit—he always liked to dress well. He would often wear a herringbone suit, not flashy but businesslike. He wore hats too. He liked Stetson hats, not the great big ones but a hat like the actor Jimmy Stewart wears in the 1940s movie *It's a Wonderful Life*. My father didn't smoke. He was usually quiet until he decided to move on something, and then he would speak his mind. He was polite and calm, but if pushed, he had a temper. One night I was

Frank Leaman

with him at the ropeworks in Dartmouth where he was overseeing the men who were tearing down the building. One of the guys started complaining because he found the work too dirty. The man threatened to report my father to authorities. Before I knew what had happened, my father had the guy by the throat and pushed up against the wall. He liked to negotiate, but he couldn't handle people whom he thought always wanted to be right.

Back in the 1950s, huge tuna fish swam off Nova Scotia. American writer Zane Grey, best known for his popular adventure novels and stories idealizing the American frontier, had a passion for fishing. Through articles he wrote for popular outdoor magazines in the 1920s and early 1930s, he promoted the place as another wild frontier.

Starting in 1937, Wedgeport, Nova Scotia, hosted the International Tuna Cup Match and became known as "the tuna fishing capital of the world." The likes of American president Franklin D. Roosevelt, author Ernest Hemingway, and Montreal Canadiens legend Jean Béliveau came to the small Acadian community in southwest Nova Scotia in pursuit of the mighty bluefin.

Tales From the Buccaneer Lodge

Philip Hooper Moore, an American mining engineer, writer, and hunting and fishing enthusiast—the man who built what would become our Buccaneer Lodge—first came to Nova Scotia to evaluate an abandoned gold mine in Queens County. Instead of finding gold, he discovered a sportsman's paradise, a vast forested area filled with big game and streams and oceans teeming with fish. By 1919, Moore had established a wilderness camp at Lowe's Landing on Lake Rossignol. Here he entertained sportsmen. He kept building and, in 1928, established what is now White Point Beach Resort in Queens County. Built originally as a hunting and fishing lodge, the resort has since been developed into one of Nova Scotia's tourism crown jewels.

Moore, who hailed from Boston and wrote poetry in his free time, ran into financial troubles at White Point, and his relationship with the lodge ended abruptly. When that happened, he worked furiously to develop Owl's Head into another White Point. From his talks with my father, we learned that he tried to extricate himself from his financial problems as he worked to promote our spot.

Frank Leaman

Moore seemed to understand the outdoors market quite well. He was a tireless promoter of sporting and wilderness trips and later helped to develop the Nova Scotia Guide's Association, making himself an officer.

Before buying the business from Moore, my father and mother (Helen neé Crowell), who were married in 1941, were guests at Owl's Head. I don't remember being there as a child, so I must have been left with my grandparents when my parents enjoyed a weekend away. I was an only child. In those days, a married couple and their children might go for a drive from Halifax and spend a night or two at a cabin, swim, and do a little fishing.

After leaving the courthouse in Chester the day of the sheriff's sale, we headed for our new purchase. We quickly realized that, although we were running seven businesses—everything from a sawmill to a salvage operation—this one was different. It was going to require a whole new level of imagination and dedication to keep our customers happy. At least we knew the area, because, at the time, we had a sawmill on Goat Lake across from Owl's Head.

Tales From the Buccaneer Lodge

Moore's old office at Owl's Head was just as he had left it. For several hundred dollars, Moore had sold all its personal belongings to my father. Moore was furious that he had lost the Buccaneer. The sheriff took almost everything.

The office was riveting. I saw things I had never thought about before. Colourful posters hung on the walls announcing fly-casting competitions for gentlemen at Owl's Head. Posters of upcoming Rod and Reel championships were everywhere. Tuna rods, lines, and all sorts of sporting paraphernalia lay around the room, waiting for action.

Copies of glossy magazines targeting wealthy Americans, with ads promoting the lodge as a destination for yachters, were on display. Chester had always been a great getaway for wealthy internationals, and Moore had a keen sense of this. Stories highlighted the ease of the Yarmouth ferry that would take American tourists to New England. We found articles written by Moore in *Field and Stream* sporting magazine and several others. I still have a signed copy of his book, *Rossignol Rhymes*. His poems describe his love for his adopted province, and when I

Frank Leaman

read them, I envision him working to make tourism great in Nova Scotia.

When we moved our things into the lodge, I found Moore's plans to turn Owl's Head into a vacation and sports mecca. The evidence of his clever engineer's mind could be seen almost everywhere I looked. He had done a magnificent drawing of an imagined fast ferry between Nova Scotia and Maine. It looked almost like a twin to the *Bluenose* ferry that sailed between Bar Harbor, Maine, and Yarmouth.

On the lodge's grounds, we found tunnels burrowing into hills. We think Moore had been looking for some mineral he suspected might be there. We don't know exactly what Moore was up to; some things were unexplainable.

In the main lodge room at Owl's Head, a sign on the back of the big wooden door stated, "This is my private residence and I am serving guests in my own home." Behind the door, an ugly club hung, to discourage rowdies. In those days, Moore saw the strict liquor laws as a hinderance to business, and this is how he got around it. We kept the sign up.

Tales From the Buccaneer Lodge

As time went on and we delved deeper into the often-unpredictable tourism business, we relied on my father; we needed him not only to discourage the rowdies but also to keep the business going. As one of our employees said, my father had 3 a.m. courage—it says a lot about the depth of a person's courage if they still have it in the early morning hours when they are alone, tired, and worn out. It says a lot if someone can keep going and make good decisions even then.

My father had great diplomacy skills. When things got chaotic, he had a peacemaker's touch. He saved many guests' holidays from disaster and smoothed the waters so that special events weren't ruined by long-remembered resentments. He showed me what it meant to be blessed as a pacifier.

Countless times, when we heard an ember of emotion break out at an organized company party, we found a way to douse the situation before it turned into a roaring flame that couldn't be stopped. Even after 35 years of being in the tourism business, we always wanted people to remember their experience at our lodge with fondness.

Frank Leaman

It wasn't just the famous potato salad, fresh lobsters, dark rum, or the sing-songs around our huge fireplace that created indelible memories for our guests; it was our interactions with them. We created relationships and friendships. I've had former guests come up to me in Dartmouth and thank me for the lovely time they had more than 30 years ago at the Buccaneer Lodge. We made people happy.

The Buccaneer Lodge and the *Buccaneer Lady*

From childhood I was captivated by the sea and our efforts to control her. The Nova Scotia coast was my teacher, along with its parade of adventurers and toilers of the sea—from fishermen to sailors, they were my main interest. How to describe a special place or building to another is a challenging, introspective task, is it not? The pages of this book are my humble attempt.

When I left Dartmouth to drive to East Chester, I felt like I was being transported into a different world. During my long days of juggling the management of several apartment rentals, a land-development company, plus running a lumberyard, I felt as though I was constantly in the midst of disputes over land or responding to customers

Frank Leaman

who demanded, "where is my lumber?" All the stress of those businesses made operating the Buccaneer Lodge feel like a vacation, even though it had its own challenges.

Running a vacation spot always looks so romantic and easy in those television advertisements which suggest that retirees give it a try. Statements like "fish and get paid for it" or "be your own boss in a holiday atmosphere" make it sound like so much fun. But then you find out the sobering truth. At our lodge there were five septic tanks, and one was always clogged. People came from New York, thought they were still in the city, and flushed all the time.

To get to our resort area from Dartmouth, you took the old highway until you saw a highway marker sign in East Chester announcing Buccaneer Road. Turning onto the dirt road, you eventually came to another road that would take you to Squid Cove, a beautiful place where people from Halifax had cottages. Next to the cottages was a mansion with a boathouse, boat launch, and a pretty boat. The mansion was never really occupied, but I heard it was owned by an American millionaire. There was an air of mystery around the place.

Tales From the Buccaneer Lodge

Back on Buccaneer Road, you'd get a magical view of Mahone Bay and the 11 acres of oceanfront that was home to our Buccaneer complex. It is no longer there but in its place is a beautiful private development called Secret Cove.

The Buccaneer consisted of eight cottages, a 12-unit motel, and the main lodge. There were four rooms in the lodge, including a spectacular dining room. A big all-encompassing room, copied or mirrored after the main room at White Point Beach Resort, overlooked Mahone Bay and was a big draw. We held weddings and company meetings there.

When we bought the Buccaneer, the main lodge was a chalet-type building made of logs and beach stone. Close by it, looking like three cubs around a mother bear, were three smaller chalet-type cottages and some outer buildings, built in the same style. Usually a light sea breeze blew across the property, just enough to make you feel lucky to be alive. Many times, I believe I heard Frank Sinatra's song "Summer Wind" as I was walking:

> *The summer wind came blowin' in from across the sea*

Frank Leaman

> *It lingered there, to touch your hair and walk with me*
> *All summer long we sang a song and then we strolled that golden sand*
> *Two sweethearts and the summer wind.*

The cottages were what you would call rustic. When you entered them, the smell of the bright wooden interior evoked for me, and I think others, a happy feeling of escape from the usual. The kind of places you don't want to leave. We had wood stoves in the cottages, which gave a feeling of going back to the land. The stove seemed to say to our guests, "If you don't fill my wood box and properly build a fire in me, you won't get warm."

All the cottages were on the beach, just like the ones in the summer movies that were popular at the time. Besides our large swimming float stationed off the beach, visitors might see a luxurious yacht visiting the area or the yacht owned by Rudy Haase, the man who became known as "Canada's great unknown environmentalist." He lived across the bay.

Tales From the Buccaneer Lodge

I can only describe the main lodge as a log palace. For me, it existed in a different dimension. We kept the huge beach-stone fireplace going all summer. The mantle above the fireplace held two sculpted tuna tails. I think they must have been 3 feet high. Tuna fishing was a big deal in the province for a time. Famous and not-so-famous people came to Nova Scotia from all over to try their hand at it—not just Ernest Hemingway.

The walls of the room were covered with rods and reels, sporting rifles, and pictures of proud sport fishermen standing with their big catches. You could feel the memories of happy times and adventure piled on top of one another. It was a place where a person needing a real getaway could rest their rushed soul. Through the room's windows, you could see our cruiser, the *Buccaneer Lady*.

The *Buccaneer Lady*

My father had a 50-foot wooden cruiser custom built by Stevens Boatworks, a traditional boatyard and marina in Chester, not far from the Buccaneer Lodge. Made of mahogany, oak, and spruce, she was the perfect boat to take our guests aboard and tour Mahone Bay and surrounding area. We called her the *Buccaneer Lady*. For our guests, our standard charter included a grand tour of Mahone Bay, Chester, and the nearby islands.

My father was the skipper of the *Buccaneer Lady*. He liked parties, so he was in his element at the helm. We hosted many office and wedding parties on board the cruiser. The *Buccaneer Lady* brought happiness to many people and was a great ambassador for Nova Scotia's beautiful ocean scenery and hospitality.

When we took over the lodge in 1956, the first thing our American guests asked for was a drink. American tourists at the Buccaneer used to look at me unbelievably when I would say, "I am sorry, we cannot serve alcohol." You should have heard the Yankees. "What?!" they responded in disbelief.

Attitudes changed and, by the late 1950s, we were given a conditional licence that allowed us to serve alcohol at a higher price than what we bought it for. This

Tales From the Buccaneer Lodge

was for the tourist industry, the idea being that it was a service for our guests. Authorities had tried to prevent shuffleboards from being brought into bars because they thought patrons would beat each other with the stones. They wanted to keep pool tables out, too, to prevent a stabbing with a cue.

Some readers may even remember a time when women were not allowed in taverns in Nova Scotia. I remember the girlfriend of a man who drove a truck in our woodlots; she dressed up as a male and snuck into a local watering hole. The trucker was a big gruff guy. His girlfriend didn't want to stay home and have him out drinking alone.

Into this bizarre arena we stepped with our request to have a bar aboard the *Buccaneer Lady*. Around this time, a tourist schooner in Newfoundland caught fire, and safety inspectors were scared. They wanted to make sure all tour vessels were safe and sound. Luckily, we were passed for a conditional licence because of our past clean record.

Our bar aboard the *Buccaneer Lady* was a big draw. The mahogany bar was located at the head of the companion way and the main lounge was in the middle of the boat. If customers wanted a drink, they would often just call down their order from the deck of the cruiser and the bartender would pass it up to them. A passenger could have a drink of navy rum for about 75 cents or $1 for a beer. Most people wanted beer.

No one was supposed to get drunk on board because that could lead to someone falling overboard, but there was a lot of drinking. We had to be careful. Liquor inspectors would come to the Buccaneer unannounced. Once someone came aboard the *Buccaneer Lady* pretending to be a guest to make sure that we were doing everything by the book. We quickly caught on to who he was and made sure we all got along.

This stanza from Lewis Carroll's poem "The Walrus and the Carpenter" reminds me of when the Nova Scotian government decided to allow alcohol to be served and sold on tour boats.

> *The time has come, the Walrus said,*
> *To talk of many things:*

Tales From the Buccaneer Lodge

Of shoes—and ships—and sealing-wax—
Of cabbages—and kings—
And why the sea is boiling hot—
And whether pigs have wings.

The Lion and the Paper Tiger

For those who are captivated by advertisements depicting the great carefree life you'll have running a tourist resort, hunting lodge, or bed and breakfast, I would like to deliver this message: unless you are prepared to go the extra mile, are an expert in diplomacy, have a big sense of humour, and an abundance of patience—don't do it.

One beautiful summer's day, we left the Buccaneer's pier for a tour of Mahone Bay. Our guests that day were on a reunion of some type. One man and woman were what you might call the odd couple. She was a large, portly woman and he was a short, slight man. I noticed his bashful manner right away. He seemed like a caricature of the stereotypical little guy who gets picked on in cartoons. The large woman seemed to be running their show. I watched her tell him where to sit and what kind of sandwich she wanted. It was like he was under her control. But their relationship wasn't any of my business; my job was to make sure they had a good, safe time.

The bar opened as we left the wharf. Drinks were served and the mood visibly changed. We had a couple of guitar players booked to play and they started the party going with couples dancing to Harry Belafonte's "Jamaica Farewell" and Patsy Cline's "Side by Side." While couples danced in the main lounge, the quiet little man started to drink the dark navy rum we had on board that day. The bartender told some jokes and the man's laughter grew louder and more animated. I noticed that his wife had one eye cocked on him like a collie dog with a sheep.

Finally, we made port on Tancook Island. The plan was to get off for a shore tour. An old half-ton truck waited for those who wished to drive around the island. Some guests decided to stay aboard the boat. What transpired next was beyond anything I had ever witnessed, and I had been on several banquet cruises where I had seen guests,

Tales From the Buccaneer Lodge

even the most seemingly sedate ones, in a fit of drunken celebration jump on the table and dance.

The quiet little man decided to stay on board. He started to sing along with our guitarists, "Down the Way Where the Nights Are Gay." In a flash, he was on the boat's stern transom. It was a small but wide rail. How he got up there so quickly, I don't know. He was singing something about dancing girls swinging to and fro when suddenly, whooidy poop, he went ass over kettle into the water.

"Harold, your teeth! Harold, your teeth!" his wife screamed.

We fished our Tarzan, soaking wet and sputtering without his false teeth, out of the water. Oh my, the screams of horror that came from his lioness about the cost of the teeth. What to do to save our client, we wondered. All that could be done was to call in the commander, the supreme problem solver—my father. Following his command, we found a scuba driver on the island. The diver agreed to a no-cure, no-pay proposal like a Lloyd's open salvage agreement (a standard form contract for a proposed marine salvage operation).

Frank Leaman

In the weedy, dark bottom of the ocean, he found our man's teeth. For a few dollars, we had restored a couple's marital bliss. We were satisfied. We had given our guests first-class treatment during an unexpected, human mini-drama. I am reminded of the saying: if you can't run with the hounds, you'd best stay on the porch.

The Diplomatic Core, Buccaneer-Style

If you want to be in the tourist, hotel, or charter business, you must be diplomatic. If you have a hot temper, forget it. Your customers are looking to you to provide them with a good time away from the stresses in their daily lives and in return you receive money to pay your bills. You need your customers and you need them to be happy. This means being flexible.

One time, a huge firm chartered the *Buccaneer Lady* to take a group of women, the wives of executives, on a tour of the Mahone Bay area while the men attended a conference. The ladies showed up with an escort, an English gentleman who tended to their every need. Off to sea we went. My father enchanted the women with the scenic views and by showing them points of interest, like the big oceanside summer homes owned by wealthy people. Then the sun was shining, the bar was open, a gentle breeze was blowing, and God was, as they say, in heaven. *Tempus fugit* or "time flies," as the Latin phrase is usually translated.

Back at the Buccaneer Lodge, the kitchen staff were preparing a lobster feast. Just as we were turning the boat back for supper, the English gentleman approached my father. The ladies wanted to stay out for at least another hour, he said. How much would it cost to make that happen? My father quickly calculated what the change in schedule would mean: the lodge's kitchen and wait staff would have to work longer and therefore be paid more, the same with the *Buccaneer Lady*'s crew, as well as the musicians who had been hired to entertain during dinner, and extra fuel costs. A longer night also meant staff would get home late and still have to do it all over again the next day. My father added all this up and gave the man a figure. It wouldn't be worth it to spoil a wonderful day all because of a few hundred dollars, the gentleman replied. It was agreed: they would stay another hour on the water and then return for their lobster supper.

Painter Jack Grey

Painter Jack Grey was a frequent and much-loved guest at the Buccaneer. Jack loved to tell stories and entertain, and he was a great pal of my father's. He was a fisherman and lived on old boats. He loved to paint the life of a fisherman, like those I grew up with, and loved to travel with us on our tours of the Tancook islands. His favourite subject for his paintings: inshore fishermen in small boats.

We all admired him, so in the earlier days of his career we gave him money to help him out. For a time, he lived on a boat in New York harbour and painted there. My father bought a complete set of his prints of the Big Apple's harbour for about $1,500. His marine scenes were done in a style that made me, as someone who loved the ocean, really feel close to his subject.

Tales From the Buccaneer Lodge

Jack's career skyrocketed. His paintings were given to American president John Kennedy and he also worked with Hollywood production companies. When he came back to Nova Scotia, he was able to have parties at the Buccaneer with 30 people and pay for all the drinks and the food. During those parties, he loved to play our piano and entertain his guests. When Jack died in Florida in 1981, we were all sad at the loss of a true Maritimer.

Lobster Pound

Henry David Thoreau might have said, "the man is richest whose pleasures are cheapest," but in more than 30 years in the tourism business and 60 years of dealing with the public, I seldom saw it that way. In my lifetime, I saw many cheapskates whose pleasures were not the cheapest but instead seemed to be in denying their family activities or food for the only reason that it cost money.

Take our lobster pound at the Buccaneer Lodge as an example. Running a lobster pound wasn't easy. After we bargained and cajoled local fishermen to sell us their catch, we had to carefully place them in our tanks with a properly maintained water temperature and circulation. It was then our job to babysit the tanks to ensure that the lobsters weren't stolen and that they got along. Lobsters are like cannibals: they will fight and kill each other. I was frequently up all night cooking lobsters before they died or for hungry guests who wanted lobster after a night of celebrating.

I learned that at 3 a.m. no price was too high for lobster. It's a different story in the cold grey morning light when any price was judged by a guest as outrageous. This was the life of an innkeeper. Having fresh lobster was a real draw for our business. I learned a few things about the allure of lobster from my old friend Clyde Henneberry, a marine painter from Eastern Passage, Nova Scotia. He also ran a lobster pound across the harbour from Halifax.

At a time when the local newspapers were full of pollution stories about Halifax harbour, Clyde pointed out that people from Halifax and Dartmouth were scared to swim in the harbour because raw sewage was being dumped there (thankfully they changed that practice). The lobsters Clyde sold also came from the harbour and, as he said, people can't get enough of them. He got a kick out of that.

Guests at the Buccaneer

We tried to help our customers however we could. One of them had become a franchisee for a cookie and baked goods company. When an executive with the company came from Montreal to check up on our friend and customer, he asked if he could set up a sales meeting on the *Buccaneer Lady*. We agreed.

We left our wharf and headed out to sea. The plan was for the Montreal executive to fly by helicopter and meet us on Little Tancook Island, where there was a government helicopter landing pad. The executive landed on the remote island in his suit and tie and, as agreed, we took him onto our boat.

"Is there a store on this island?" he asked.

Frank Leaman

"It's only a small one for the locals," he was told.

"Well, let's see if they have any of our cookies," the executive replied.

Little did he know that two days before, we had visited the store and planted some cookies there. What a surprise the executive had when he found the little store well stocked.

"That's distribution!" he declared. We had learned quickly how to cater to our clients' every need.

Another night a big shot from an American company rented the hall in the Buccaneer Lodge for a sales meeting. The customer decided he wanted lobsters, but not from the pound. He wanted them caught, and as quickly as possible, cooked and on the table. We obliged. One of our staff slipped out of the lodge and hid some lobsters from our pound in the flat-bottomed rowboat that was tied to our swim float.

Later in the day, the big shot, along with his guests, watched as our staff made their way to the rowboat to catch their dinner. Our little prank went off smoothly and fresh lobster was brought back to be boiled. Luckily, nobody noticed the rubber band that had mistakenly been left on a claw. Robert Lewis Stephenson knew what he was talking about when he said, "Everyone lives by selling something."

Getting back to how we figure out the true cost of our pleasurers, I will relate this story. One day tied to the wharf on Tancook Island we saw a longline fishing boat that looked as though it had been badly mauled by the sea. Our guide told us it had come in from offshore, where it was fishing for halibut. The tail end of an ugly storm had caught the longliner and almost finished it off. When the fisherman came ashore, he sat by a woodstove all night smoking and drinking rum. He hardly talked and just sat with what some call the "thousand-mile stare." After such a close call, what could the halibut he caught be worth? What price should they charge for it? People always want to know the price of things. What price should the fisherman get for risking his life?

I'm reminded of when I took people on tours of Oak Island. The place has lured treasure hunters since the late 1700s, spurred by rumours that Captain William Kidd's treasure was buried there. Countless men have paid a hefty price for their obsession with Oak Island—not only with their money but, for some, with their lives.

Our Neighbours at the Buccaneer

The *Buccaneer Lady* was under repair. A part on her old diesel engine needed to be replaced. We worked diligently not to slip any of the oil in the bilges into the cove. We knew we had a watchful eye on us, and we were scared. Our next-door neighbour was one of Canada's top environmentalists. Around the Buccaneer we always had fascinating people who cast long reaches around the world.

Often called the "godfather of land conservation" in Nova Scotia, Rudy Haase was our neighbour and customer. He was a giant in his field. If you had a piece of timberland and wanted to sell, Rudy would buy it on the spot, not to sell the wood but to preserve it. I know because I sold him a lot and he did just that.

Rudy was born in the United States but came to Canada and dedicated his life to protecting the natural world. He founded Friends of Nature in 1954, and through his work helped to preserve key landscapes not only in Nova Scotia and Maine but also in New Zealand and Costa Rica. Celebrated in the province, his work earned him the Order of Nova Scotia. He died in 2017 at the age of 95.

Cyrus Eaton was another good friend and client at the Buccaneer. He was born in 1883 in Pugwash, a village on Nova Scotia's Northumberland Strait, and went on to develop gas utilities in western Canada. He was also focused on investment banking and the steel industry. By the 1920s, he was the controlling shareholder in Goodyear Tire and Rubber.

Cyrus lost most of his fortune during the Great Depression before making a comeback during the 1940s and 1950s in the railroad industry. In 1955, inspired by a manifesto issued by philosopher Bertrand Russell and Albert Einstein highlighting the dangers posed by nuclear weapons and the need for peaceful resolutions to international conflicts, Cyrus offered to hold an international conference of intellectuals and scientists.

Frank Leaman

In 1957, the first Pugwash Conference on Science and World Affairs was held in his hometown.

During the Cold War, Cyrus wanted world peace and made friends with communists: this made him a controversial figure. I remember when he brought Yuri Gagarin, the Soviet Air Forces pilot and cosmonaut who became the first human to journey into outer space, to Nova Scotia. The anger was high—it was at the height of the Cold War and people were suspicious of Russians.

Cyrus's beautiful wooden home, designed by architect Andrew Cobb, and his pristine property at Deep Cove, across the bay from us on the Aspotogan Peninsula, were treasures to behold. Although he had many other properties, including his farms in the United States, he chose for his ashes to be buried at Deep Cove.

He loved Mahone Bay and admired it for its beauty and cleanliness. He recognized our place and Mahone Bay as an earthly paradise to be respected. This man, like most of our neighbours and clients, understood the dangers of pollution.

I only ever saw Cyrus standing on his pier. He would

never come to the Buccaneer. Sometimes he would charter the *Buccaneer Lady* for his guests, but we would go over to his pier and pick them up and take them on a cruise. Our interactions with his staff were always cordial. He was an old man when we knew him. Whenever he needed to rent one of our cottages or charter our boat, we were there.

Cyrus Eaton and Rudy Haase were good customers. They understood the need to protect the province's coast and its wild inhabitants long before I did. A whaling station in Blandford, when it was operational, always seemed to have whales up on the beach ready for processing. The oil from the whales was used in lubricants, detergents, and soaps. The whale meat and bone were used mostly for pet food and livestock feed. Our boat tours by the station brought mixed reaction from our customers. In 1972, the federal government put a halt to commercial whaling in Canada. I think it was the activists who chased these practices out of the area.

Frank Leaman

Caesar's Head

So many interesting people came to us at the Buccaneer, I can't possibly remember them all. One such guest was Dr. S. Laufer of Halifax. He was an esteemed doctor of internal medicine and one of the earliest specialists in his field in the province. In his book *A Lucky Life*, Dr. Richard Goldbloom describes Dr. Laufer as "short and balding, with tufts of hair projecting laterally from behind his ears. He spoke English with a fairly pronounced Germanic accent. He sounded like a caricature of Sigmund Freud."

From his mansion in Chester, Dr. Laufer brought us fascinating visitors who enjoyed charters on the *Buccaneer Lady*. Wherever I went, I met people who knew him; they spoke highly of both his medical skills and his philanthropic work. I can attest to his medical skills because he became my doctor too and saved me from many health scares.

One of the places Dr. Laufer raised money for was Bonny Lea Farm in Chester. Started in 1973, the farm provides a place where adults with intellectual disabilities can live and work. He would call wealthy people he knew and ask them to donate money or to help in some other way. From Dr. Laufer, I learned that I too could help to solve problems in our society and how important it was to develop a love for the needy. His interest in the arts was also well known and respected.

A room at the Art Gallery of Nova Scotia is named after him. It is filled with treasures that he donated. One of those treasurers is a marble bust called *Head of the Emperor Augustus*. Dr. Laufer was said to have bought it in Italy. Before he donated it to the art gallery, it was in his doctor's office on Oxford Street in Halifax. Whenever I went there, I took comfort from this marble bust that measured 29 by 22 by 24 centimetres and its antiquity. I remember when this office was being painted; everything was upset and out of order. A painter hit the pedestal by mistake and the bust rolled across the floor. The doctor went out of control. "Oh my God!" he yelled in despair, asking the man if he knew how valuable the piece of art was. Did he know that Augustus was considered the greatest Roman emperor and ruled while Jesus Christ was alive?

"That old thing. I wouldn't give you a case of beer for that," the painter replied.

"If the glories of Rome don't move you, I guess they don't," I thought when I heard this story. When the hound dog goes hunting with the men, does he have to know how the shotguns work? When Dr. Laufer died, it was a sad day. He loved the Buccaneer and its history. I salute him for all the good he did in his life.

The Late-night Innkeeper

There is an old Maritime song I am reminded of that says if you're "a stuffed shirt" or a "fuss pot," you had better stay away from certain occupations. Being an innkeeper, I would say, is one of them. The job requires that you meet each person, in whatever place they are in their lives, at that moment in time. It requires that you're flexible and able to live with unpredictability—if you can't do that, you won't last.

We had budgetary constraints at the Buccaneer, so that meant as the owner/boss I often worked alone at

Tales From the Buccaneer Lodge

night, and I was forced to deal with whatever situation might arise. On one of those nights I was awakened by a noise I instinctively knew was trouble. My bedside clock told me it just after 3 a.m. That hour, my mind recalled, was popular for out-of-control incidents. As the person in charge, I realized that any decision I made would affect the income of my family and our employees. I could be sued if a customer thought I made a bad decision.

From my big window upstairs, I had a prominent view of the lodge's main yard. I usually slept by the window so that I could see most of the Buccaneer's property. It was a great vantage point. On that summer night, I looked out the second-storey window and thought I saw two naked figures chasing each other, yelling in what sounded like both fear and anger. From experience, I could distinguish the difference between screams of laughter and screams that told me they were expressing genuine fear. The screams I heard that night were the latter. I decided to investigate. I was afraid to call the Mounties, because if there was a scene and rumours spread, our business could get a bad reputation.

Frank Leaman

I dressed, went downstairs, and grabbed my watchman's flashlight. When I opened the front door, the two figures ran toward the wharf. In the soft light of the moon and a lamp on the wharf, I could make out the silhouettes of a naked man and a naked woman. It appeared he was running for his life. She ran after him, screaming in anger about the horrible things she would do to him after he was caught. My mind, still heavy with sleep, finally told me this scene wasn't a dream; it was real. I realized that the couple were not only regular guests at the Buccaneer but two prominent people in the province. They were politicians.

Earlier in the day there had been a cruise and party aboard the *Buccaneer Lady*. Aside from the usual social interactions, I recalled an incident that offered a clue as to why this explosive incident might now be taking place. The gentleman in my immediate view had been publicly accused of flirting, and other more serious charges, with another lady guest. Such accusations weren't uncommon at social gatherings on the boat and I had hoped the disagreement would pass. Now, several hours later, I saw that it hadn't passed and had instead turned into a

Tales From the Buccaneer Lodge

full-blown, dangerous scene involving two naked people chasing each other across a dimly lit public space. I knew that the scene could quickly turn disastrous.

The couple appeared to be doing a dance based on the nursery rhyme "Ring around the Rosy" around the lodge's main building. Inspiration struck. Number One cottage was near the front door of the main lodge. I knew it was empty. I saw that the naked runners were about to turn by the lobster pound, and I knew had to act fast. Number One was an older cottage, small but strongly built, with few windows. I ran over to it and opened the front door.

In the dark, I waited. Before long, the terrified man was close by, in all his naked glory, not looking a bit like the officious man he was during the day. I yelled to him: "In here and quickly!" He practically jumped in and managed to bolt the door shut just before she came running at it like a battering ram. She screamed and cursed like a sailor, but the door wouldn't budge. Her venom and fury raged; the bolt held firm. Finally, like an ocean tide, she turned. It got very quiet. The man sat on the bed breathing deeply like he was steam engine. He covered himself with a blanket, and I gave him some of my clothes. He was drunk and talked and talked about his life and his awkward predicament. The woman, he told me, was not his wife, but his lover.

At dawn, we dared to open the door. There was no one in sight. He made it to his car, found the key he had hidden under the fender and fled. The woman disappeared in the morning before I could talk to her. Later, my body shook when I thought about what could have happened. I was reminded of what a champion boxing friend once told me: the best way to take a punch is not to be where it lands. My actions that night, I felt, proved this. If the naked lovers' squabble had resulted in a tragic fall or an assault, the media would have had a field day.

We weren't called the "Lover's Paradise" for no reason.

The Moose Is Loose

The story I am about to relate is true. Well, it is supposed to be true. It was told to me by a conservationist who wishes to remain anonymous. He was so passionate about protecting the environment and its non-human inhabitants that he was beyond Gandhi in his dedication and the fierceness of his convictions. You didn't dare drop a piece of litter on the ground in front of him. All he talked about was garbage and the harm plastics were doing to the environment. He was hateful if he thought you were doing something against the environment.

The Buccaneer was famous from the time it was built as a place to go for hunting and fishing. I remember a sign that hung in a diner in Chester: "Man is always trying to outwit trout, racehorses, and women." It was true: the people who hired our boats and stayed at our lodge were passionate about fish and game and loved to plan and scheme about how they were going to catch tuna and swordfish and hunt moose.

After tuna, the big prize for outdoorsmen was moose. People would come from all over the world to track down the creatures. But the province's conservation officers were worried about Nova Scotia's moose population. Believing it was dropping dangerously, they started a program

Frank Leaman

called Operation Crossroad. Part of the plan was putting in place a decoy moose—called Bullwinkle, after the cartoon character—which did a good job of pretending to be a real moose. The conservationist told me that a hunter opened fire on poor Bullwinkle. The decoy moose was repaired and put back on the job in a different spot. It was fired on again and the shooter was caught. The conservationist told me Bullwinkle made them quite a bit of money. The fines were steep, but the hunter's desire for the thrill of getting a rack was stronger. I always thought a less dangerous pursuit than hunting might be darts or golf. But my conservationist friend reminded me that people will fly as far as Africa to hunt big game animals. It was Raymond, one of our guides at the Buccaneer, who used to say, "The Lord's bounty may not be for sale, but the Devil's is."

Butterbox Babies

It still eats at me after all these years. About a mile and a half down the road from the Buccaneer was a place

Tales From the Buccaneer Lodge

known as "the baby farm." The farm was closed a few years before we bought the resort property, but as a child I knew of it and always wondered what went on there. I was told that nothing ever happened at the farm, but that I should not go near it because it was haunted. That was all I was told. I listened and didn't question what I heard. Those were the times.

When I got older, I did some research and found out that the farm was called the Ideal Maternity Home. Operated by William and Lila Young from the late 1920s to the 1940s, the home started as a place where local married couples could find good maternity care, and unwed mothers could go to have their babies discreetly, often before giving them up for adoption. Some women at the home were wrongly told that their baby had died. They found out later they had been lied to. Their babies were alive, but they had no idea where they were.

A system was in place so that American couples could travel to Nova Scotia to adopt from the Ideal Maternity Home. I have heard that some couples paid up to $10,000 for a baby. Sometimes the home had as many as 100

Frank Leaman

babies available for adoption, according to a group of survivors who conducted research on the home's history. I tried, but failed to understand how people could do such a horrible thing for money.

If you were ugly, had health issues, or had the wrong skin colour, the homeowners considered you unadoptable and left you to die. They buried you in the woods behind the home or buried you at sea. The babies became known as "Butterbox Babies" because small pine butterboxes from the local dairy were used as coffins. They were the right size for a newborn. Every week the truck from LaHave Creamery would pull into our lane to drop off milk, cream, and butter in the same type of wooden boxes used for those unwanted babies. I feel duped thinking about those boxes now and not having known the true story about the farm.

Back then, the baby farm was often defended as a good business because it was said to be good for the economy in East Chester. On the other hand, nobody dared talk about the place and what really went on there until years after it closed. Sometimes people who had been born at the farm would show up at the Buccaneer as adults because they were in the area looking for their parents. They were deeply affected by their experience there. They needed answers. The survivors I talked to were hurt, very hurt.

One man told me he felt that he had been rejected by his mother, not once, but twice.

"What do you mean?" I asked him.

"My mother left me with strangers at the farm and walked away," he said. "After years of searching, I found my mother when I was an adult. When I called her, she told me to never call her again. She hadn't told her husband about me and didn't plan to. I was rejected for a second time in my life by my birth mother."

Some survivors of the home had committed suicide or had had nervous breakdowns. Birth records existed with parents' names on them, but children weren't allowed to see them. They were told that they weren't allowed to search for their parents. The home is long gone, but in East Chester there is a monument dedicated to the babies born there. They haven't been forgotten.

Tancook Island and the Island of Mystery

The Ghost Ship and Oak Island

Many stories are told about ghost ships, buried treasure, and strange occurrences circling around the islands in Mahone Bay. It's hard to believe, but some say there are as many as 350 islands in the bay.

Guests aboard the *Buccaneer Lady* repeatedly asked about *Young Teazer*, a 60-foot American privateer schooner and possibly the most famous ghost ship off the coast of Nova Scotia. It is said to appear as a phantom burning ship, known as the Teazer Light, in the waters between Mahone Bay and Chester.

I had some silver Louis XIV coins that came from the

French ship *Chameau* or *Le Chameau*. That ship transported passengers and supplies to New France, but near the end of her last voyage, a storm blew her onto some rocks off Cape Breton Island in late August of 1725. She sank.

In 1965, Alex Storm and his associates located the wreckage near Chameau Rock, off Louisbourg, and recovered a treasure of gold and silver pieces. I bought the coins through Storm, who has become Nova Scotia's famous treasure hunter. When I showed our guests the coins, they always asked, "Why not some coins from *Young Teazer*?"

"Well," I told them, "we took dive teams to the so-called secret site of the wreck, which was believed to be off Snake Island, about 15 nautical miles from Owl's Head in Mahone Bay, but our divers reported no luck."

Our curious tourists had to content themselves with a wooden cross, made from a piece of the *Young Teazer*'s keel. It now rests inside St. Stephen's Anglican Church in Chester. Much of the wreckage was salvaged, including some timbers that were used in the Rope Loft pub and restaurant located on Chester's harbour. A piece of the ship's keel and a cane made from *Teazer* fragments are also at the Maritime Museum of the Atlantic in Halifax.

The *Young Teazer* was a fast privateer schooner and raided many ships, including several at the mouth of Halifax harbour. My research discovered that she was eventually chased by several ships of the British Royal Navy. HMS *La Hogue*, a 74-gun ship led the pursuit. She was eventually cornered in Mahone Bay, according to information from the Maritime Museum of the Atlantic. As the British approached her, she blew up, killing most of the crew on board. According to folklore, the ship is often seen at night on fire, on the horizon. The sightings have happened regularly near the site of the explosion on or near the anniversary of June 27. Nova Scotia's famous folklorist Helen Creighton collected several versions of the story in her book *Bluenose Ghosts*. She also noted that many of the sightings could have been optical illusions that occurred during a full moon.

I saw an apparition that might have been the *Young Teazer*. It happened one night when we encountered St. Elmo's Fire on board the *Buccaneer Lady*. We were returning from Tancook Island. It was dark, except for the moonlight. Suddenly, it looked as though there was fire everywhere and little droplets that sparkled like diamonds. Off in the distance, I could see the image of a burning ship.

I researched St. Elmo's Fire for more details, and since I'm not a scientist, I'll leave my explanation brief. Here's what I found: it's a weather phenomenon that involves a gap in electrical charge. It's like lightning, but it's not. And it's not fire. Long ago when it got its name, the phenomenon sometimes appeared to ships at sea during thunderstorms. Its glowing ball of light awed sailors, who took it as a good omen.

Tancook Island

The Tancook islands were always a source of wonder to me, and to our guests. Big Tancook Island is the largest of the islands in Mahone Bay. Sitting at the outer edge of the bay, facing the open sea, it is about 4 kilometres in length and less than half that in width, forming a rough

Tales From the Buccaneer Lodge

C shape or the shape of a fishhook. As its name suggests, Little Tancook Island is the smaller of the two islands but still the second largest island in Mahone Bay. It is only 1.5 kilometres long and 1 kilometre wide and is separated from Big Tancook Island by a wide strait called "The Chops."

The guides we had on board the *Buccaneer Lady* were mostly Tancookers and had uncanny ways of finding fish for our guests. Of course, for generations their families had lived on the island. One of our guides was an old fisherman of about 60. He looked like a sea captain in his black peacoat, white cap, work pants, and a cigarette hanging out of his mouth. He seemed to be able to smell weather changes. He told me his arthritis acted as his weather gauge. Before we had radar on the boat, he showed me how to use a watch and compass to navigate by time, cardinal directions, and the tides. He and our other guides saved our lives more than a few times in the fog. We made it home alive and, thank God, we never lost a client at sea.

My father got on well with the captains on Tancook Island. They were independent and always carried around

Frank Leaman

huge wads of cash in their pockets. They had customs and ways of doing things that came from way back, passed down through the generations. At that time, most of their fishing boats were open decked. Some looked as though the family's doghouse had been taken from the yard and placed on the deck of the boat. It was a primitive way to give those on board the boat a place to stand in foul weather and save them from freezing to death. Many of the boats on the island were what they called "one-lungers," referring to their one-cylinder make-and-break engines. These boats sparked along on their noisy putt-putt engines. One benefit of the old engines was if your hands were freezing, you could put them over the exhaust for warmth.

When they weren't out in their boats, the Tancookers showed me the floating tubs they used for duck hunting. Looking at them, I knew they meant business. Anchored in a favourite hunting spot, a hunter would hide in the tub until he heard birds coming. When the moment was ripe, he opened fire to get what would become Sunday's dinner. I never got in the tubs, but I used to like watching others hunt in them.

Tales From the Buccaneer Lodge

I liked these good, island folk. We liked to joke, and they kept me laughing. One time on the Tancook wharf we saw cages full of cats being loaded onto a ferry that was en route to the mainland.

"What's going on?" I asked.

"Well, Frankie boy, the island was getting overrun by cats, so we made a deal with the vet ashore."

"What deal?" I asked.

"All these cats will be fixed so as not to have kittens," they told me.

Someone piped up, "Just lock them up at night."

"They does it in the daytime as well as the nighttime," I told them.

The Oak Island Mystery

Decades ago, I took people on tours of Oak Island, which continues to intrigue people today with its mystery. The strange saga of the search for the Oak Island treasure continues. Since the 19th century, many attempts have

Frank Leaman

been made to find buried treasure on the island, but no significant treasure site has ever been found. Is it not true that more money has been put in the ground to hunt for gold than has ever come out? I don't think there are any treasures there.

My part of the tour involved taking people ashore on Oak Island and showing them the money pit and the tunnel. According to the earliest theory, the pit held a pirate treasure buried by Captain William Kidd, a Scottish ship's captain, privateer, and pirate. His life ended after he was tried and executed for piracy when he returned from a voyage to the Indian Ocean.

First, I took visitors from the Buccaneer Lodge on the *Tuna Finn*, the 35-foot wooden cruiser we bought from the Armdale Yacht Club in Halifax, and later on the *Buccaneer Lady*. There was a small wharf on Oak Island where we would tie up and then walk to the "money pit"—the original shaft on the site that was dug by early explorers. For a time, there was a little museum on the island. A woman showed up and I think we would give her $4 to have a look around.

Tales From the Buccaneer Lodge

For over 200 years, people have looked for treasure on Oak Island, and they are still looking. What drives them when fortunes and lives are lost in deep disappointment? As many as six men are reported to have died in efforts to find the treasure.

Robert Restall tried to get my family to invest money in his quest to find treasure on the island. Restall, his teenage son, and his treasure-hunting partner, Karle Graeser, went to the island in the late 1950s after getting permission from one of the property owners. Robert told my father that he was only feet away from the treasure and, when he found it, he would share some of it with him. My father didn't believe him.

Nothing went according to Robert's plan. They dug a deep shaft. I remember how primitive his equipment looked. He went underground and didn't come up. He was overcome by hydrogen sulfide fumes. His son then went down the shaft and lost consciousness. Karle and another man tried to save the two men but died in the heroic attempt.

I am still mystified by Oak Island. People I have long admired told me not to dismiss what can become a treasure-

Frank Leaman

seeking addiction. I did not like the driven madness of some seekers who looked like they had been possessed by incredibly wild tales. But I tried to be respectful. I felt I had seen the madness of "gold fever."

Over the years, various strangers came to me, asking me to let them use a metal detector on the grounds around the Buccaneer Lodge. They said they knew a treasure was buried there too, and they would split it with me when it was found. These treasure-trove stories were too common in the Mahone Bay area.

I did discover tunnels at the Buccaneer Lodge. Some people said there was treasure buried there, but I think the tunnels were built so they could take mud out of the ground and use it for making paint.

I know there are real buried treasurers in the world. I held in my hands silver coins that were recovered from the shipwreck of *Le Chameau*. For years people didn't believe treasure from *Le Chameau* would ever be found—but it was. Who am I to say whether treasure will ever be found on Oak Island? For us, the place was a good tourist draw. It was good for business. Yup, it was.

Tales From the Buccaneer Lodge

The Mysterious Stone

One night I sat in a drinking establishment in Dartmouth. It was getting late and I was feeling cozy, not wanting to go home. A man sat across from me, the brew he was drinking starting to show on his tired face.

"Would you tell me that story again from the beginning?" I asked the workman, who was holding his beer glass in his calloused hands. "I will keep the beer coming."

"Well," he said. "We were hired to find the mystery stone."

"Where were you looking?" I asked.

"At the Creighton House in Dartmouth. The mystery stone is said to tell you how to get the Oak Island gold."

Previously, this mystery stone was said to have kicked around Halifax at Creighton's bookbindery. The stone was eventually said to have landed at Evergreen House, once home to folklorist Helen Creighton. Today, Evergreen House is a historic home open to the public and home to the Dartmouth Heritage Museum.

The workman's story seemed fantastic to me. I am a

member of the Evergreen Writers Group, and we meet regularly at Evergreen House. One day, after I heard his story, I found myself looking out some windows in the back of the house and seeing large piles of granite stones. I learned that a stone wall had been taken down. Crew members of a TV show about the Oak Island treasure had been there to check on the story. The mystery stone was apparently never found, but the museum did gain free landscaping as a result of the search.

I don't think the stone exists. But many people believe that it does. Maybe it is our own version of the Loch Ness monster, the large marine creature believed by some to inhabit Loch Ness, Scotland, and by others to be nothing more than a myth.

Tales From the Buccaneer Lodge

The *Buccaneer Lady*.

Life around the Dartmouth Pier

The Dartmouth Pier

If you stand in the parking lot of Alderney Landing on the Dartmouth waterfront and look toward the Angus L. Macdonald Bridge connecting Halifax and Dartmouth, you will see a long finger-shaped pier of earth, rocks, and boulders that was once known as the Dartmouth pier. From the time I was a young boy, I was fascinated with the marine traffic that tied up to the pier. Eventually, I became the wharfinger or record keeper for the pier. I recorded every ship and barge that stopped there and made note of how long they stayed. My job was to send those records to the harbour authority so that they could

Frank Leaman

charge wharfage, a fee for using the pier. I didn't fully appreciate then what adventure and tales from the high seas would come into my life.

Marine traffic was constant in those days, including freighters from Europe and other parts of the world. Some came to pick up wooden pit props or small logs used in mining operations; other freighters came to pick up or deliver cargo. They waited at the Dartmouth pier until a berth came available across the harbour in Halifax. Many ships from the sealing fleet, like the *North Star, Arctic Prowler,* and *Olaf Neilson,* came by too. Other times, huge ocean-going tugs came and stayed while they waited for their tows to be prepared. I remember one tug arrived from Poland to tow a surplus naval frigate to La Spezia, Italy.

We also had a large following of Dartmouth folk who visited the pier to swim, fish, and paint harbour scenes. It wasn't uncommon for locals to keep a small fishing craft or recreational boat there to use on a fine summer's day.

On shore, at the head of the pier, stood my family's lumber company and woodworking mill called Dartmouth

Tales From the Buccaneer Lodge

Woodworkers and Builders Supplies—back in those days, long names were in fashion. We had a two-storey wooden building that looked like it had been built during the war. Inside, we had a few offices overlooking the harbour. They were not palatial, but they were nice. I could look out the windows and see everything that was going on. It was a perfect spot to watch the pier. We worked every day except Sunday. On Sundays, we still had to come by to inspect the place to make sure there weren't any break-ins or people sleeping in the building.

Our mill property formerly belonged to Frederick Scarfe, who was mayor of the Town of Dartmouth from 1889 to 1892. He ran a company there that made sashes, doors, and other building supplies.

When my father bought the mill, it was still full of woodworking equipment. The lot on which the mill stood was called a pre-Confederation water lot. Regulations allowed property owners to build up to 300 feet into the harbour. I remember going out in a rowboat with my father to pick up logs and timbers that had washed up along the shore to build cribwork to expand our

Frank Leaman

property. We expanded it into the harbour and filled it with rocks.

It was a different time then. We did some foolish things that we would never do today. Our sawmill produced copious amounts of shavings. We sold some to farmers to use as bedding for their livestock, but the shavings still piled up high. When someone suggested that we "let the shavings go on the outgoing tide," we foolishly agreed. Before we knew it, an irate employee of the Dartmouth Ferry Commission informed us that one of the harbour ferryboats had sucked in some of the shavings and this had caused considerable trouble to the engine. Sufficiently chastised, we never sent the shavings out with the tide again.

Getting back to the pier, it was a busy time when I was wharfinger. Railroad tracks went out onto the pier and could shunt boxcars. Local car dealers would bring in new cars on the trains and a boxcar might have three new cars on wood staging inside. I remember watching them disassemble the wooden contraption and wondering who could afford a beautiful new car. Today when I visit the huge autoport down the road in Eastern Passage, I think of how simple things used to be. The autoport is considered one of North America's largest vehicle processing and transshipment facilities, handling almost 185,000 vehicles every year.

When bigger cargo containers started coming into the harbour, they stopped at special container terminals. The Dartmouth pier became a holding area for smaller vessels. The day the maritime tugs brought SS *Bear* up to the pier my eyes were opened wide to history. It was the early 1960s, and when I looked at her record, I could not believe she was in front of me. She radiated historic adventure. When I look at something from another century, I am often awestruck. I get a feeling that this is something special, something that has survived the tough test of time. The ship's designs made it almost look like an apparition, a ghost ship. But she wasn't; she was real.

Bear

Bear was probably the most famous ship in the United States Coast Guard's history. A dual steam-powered and sailing ship, *Bear* had 15-centimetre-thick sides, which helped her on her exploits in the Arctic and Antarctic. She was considered a forerunner of today's modern icebreakers.

Starting life in 1874 as a Scottish sealer, she worked out of Newfoundland before taking part in major historic events such as the search for the storied Greely Expedition in the mid-1880s. As the history books tell it, 25 men set sail for the far north to collect scientific data about the Arctic. Three years later, on August 1, 1884, a rescue vessel carrying First Lieutenant Adolphus Greely and only five other remaining survivors of the Lady Franklin Bay Expedition pulled into the harbour of Portsmouth, New Hampshire.

Bear had not only been to the Arctic but to Antarctica with Admiral Richard Byrd. She also had many adventures in Alaska with Captain Michael "Hell Roaring" Healy, the first man of African-American descent to command a ship of the United States government. *Bear* patrolled 32,000 kilometres of Alaskan coastline. The son of a slave, Healy was known to have deep sympathy for

Tales From the Buccaneer Lodge

Alaska's Indigenous peoples. He hated the bootleggers who abused them. When he saw that commercial fishing had depleted the whale and seal populations and that the Indigenous residents of the area were threatened with starvation, he decided to do something bold. With the help of Sheldon Jackson, a Presbyterian minister and powerful missionary who preached the Word all over Alaska, Healy helped introduce reindeer from Siberia to Alaska as a source of food and clothing. My friend, who worked all over the Arctic, saw the reindeer. He said the herds had become huge and helped the local people.

Bear was also a movie star. She starred in the 1930 film version of American author Jack London's adventure novel *The Sea-Wolf*. In 1944, the US Navy decommissioned *Bear* and a few years later my father's friend Captain Frank Shaw of Shaw Steamship Company in Halifax bought her for a reported $5,199. Captain Shaw repaired *Bear* and had plans to take her to Newfoundland to take part in sealing. But the industry was changing, and repairs proved costly, so she spent several years sitting idle. In the early 1960s she was sold to Alfred Johnson. He wanted to turn her into a floating restaurant in Philadelphia. Our lumber firm would play a part in her transformation.

The shipyard gave us contracts for planking and woodworking to prepare *Bear* for her trip to Philadelphia. The shipyards knew we could find much of the tough-to-get lumber for vessels. They knew we had some Douglas fir logs, which they wanted for crosstrees. Crosstrees are the two horizontal spars at the upper ends of the topmasts of sailing ships. In the old days, they would say that a sailor was a top man because he climbed to the top of the mast. *Bear* had a sailing rig as well as engines.

This was a high old time for Alfred Johnson. He had a yacht built and, while he waited for the work to be done on *Bear*, he sailed his new yacht, dubbed *Little Bear*, around Nova Scotia. Everything seemed to be going according to his plan until the boss at the shipyard's carpentry shop sunk his jackknife into the old planking on *Bear*'s hull. "She's finished," he declared. To fully repair her would cost too much money.

I knew the Atlantic Ocean was a vicious force when angry. With my own eyes I had seen the planks of many ships ripped up like straw, and sometimes the ships never returned from their adventures. I well remember one time climbing into the after-hold of a sealer to get an invoice signed. Standing at the bottom of the ship's ladder, I looked up and saw daylight shining through the deck above.

Alfred didn't seem to listen to the carpenter at the shipyard. When the work was done on the old *Bear*, she left Halifax harbour in 1969; aboard her were two brothers who were experienced seamen. The tug *Irving Birch* towed her because her engines weren't working. Off the coast of Yarmouth, they hit a big squall, and as the carpenter in the shipyard had predicted, she started to take on water. About 160 kilometres east of Cape Sable Island, she sank.

Bear was about 90 years old at the time of her sinking and the *Irving Birch* tried hard to save her but, sadly, the work of our company and the shipyard went to the bottom. No crew was lost, but a legend was.

Over the years I've often thought of her. Memories came flooding back when I visited the Dartmouth Heritage

Museum and the Maritime Museum of the Atlantic in Halifax and I admired the model ships they have of her.

Arctic Prince

Looking at an aerial photo of Halifax harbour in 1967, I see it is filled with ships. A naval review is taking place in celebration of Canada's centennial. In the far-left corner of the picture, I see our lumberyard. It shows its close relationship to the old Dartmouth pier. You can mark it by the white office building. Alongside the pier is our oil tanker, ex-Imperial *LaHave*. Her job had once been to go around the harbour, pull up alongside the ships, and fill them with fuel. When she became surplus, my father bought her from Imperial Oil. We used her for about five years as an extension to our lumberyard, a storage space for our lumber.

When the railway eventually bought our land, we sold *LaHave* to Partridge Motor Boat Service. They used her as salvage. People came from all over the world to buy parts for her engine.

Tales From the Buccaneer Lodge

In the 1967 photo, you can also see the hulk of an old boat called *Arctic Prince*. Our friend Captain Shaw bought her and kept her at the pier. She gave me a shock one afternoon. Most days I would go home for a warm lunch. At my house on Creighton Street, my wife would have a nice lunch waiting for me, like soup and sandwiches. I was only 21 years old when we married. We would go on to raise five children. One day during lunch, my wife answered the phone. "Mr. Leaman, Mr. Leaman, your oil tanker just rolled over and sank!"

I was glad it wasn't our oil tanker. As far as I know, she's still there under the water.

Cruising for Timber

Our mill supplied wooden ships with the timber they needed for repairs. We supplied ships from the sealing fleet, like the *North Star, Arctic Prowler, Olaf Neilson,* and countless other schooners and workboats. We'd get a call that they needed, say, a ship's knee—for the joints

Frank Leaman

and pressure points of the vessel. This could be where the side of the ship bends up in the bow. We would have to go into the woods, dig up a root, and find the perfect, naturally curved piece of wood.

Usually this meant we'd drive to our tree lot in Lunenburg County and find large roots and parts of hardwood trees. For the hardwood, you could get good money. Aside from the land in Dartmouth, we had land around Chester. The land in Chester was wild space, except for Goat Lake, where we had a sawmill.

When it came to lumber, my job was to drive the truck and get the receipts signed. I also had a licence to grade lumber because the government had decided that lumber had to be graded by a professional lumber grader.

Cruising for lumber took place in the spring and fall. I spent a lot of time cruising woodlots trying to make a good decision. I didn't bring a forester with me to help; instead, I would bring a special character who most often chewed tobacco and had the innate ability to look up toward the sky and say, "This is the tree we want."

We might walk in the woods for as many as four hours

before we found the right tree. We didn't use anything more sophisticated than a tree measuring stick, an old-fashioned tool that required no calculator. The tool looked like a short wooden yardstick, but with different markings on it. It was most often used for measuring the diameter of a tree. We also had another tool from Norway that you could stick into the tree to determine its quality. But really when it came down to it, you had to rely on your own instincts.

Governor Cornwallis

One of my father's customers at the mill, before I was old enough to be working full time, was a man named Hugh Weagle, or as we knew him, Hughie. When I was a boy of about 10, my grandfather took me down to Elliott Street in Dartmouth, where we met the Weagle family. Hughie was well known around Dartmouth for his skill as a boat builder. His shop was on the waterfront, where King's Wharf is now located. He built small boats and barges.

Frank Leaman

One day he got a contract to build a ferry boat to take passengers and cars across the Halifax harbour. Everyone said he couldn't do it, that the job was too big, but Hughie did it. The ferry was called the *Governor Cornwallis*.

On November 20, 1941, she was launched. But her working life was cut short: just over three years after she was launched, she left Halifax on December 22, 1944, with cars and several hundred passengers aboard her, when her crew discovered a fire in the engine room. Fire engines and fire boats couldn't put out the fire. Consumed by fire, the *Governor Cornwallis* was towed to Georges Island in Halifax harbour, and beached. She later disappeared into the deep water.

My Father's Lightship

Most of the lightships have long disappeared. Many books have been written about Nova Scotia's lighthouses and the men and women who kept a light on in the darkness to help marine traffic navigate the province's rocky shores. But not as much is known about lightships. Also known as lightvessels, these special ships acted as floating lighthouses in dangerous places. At one time, you could find several along the Nova Scotia coastline. They were mostly used in waters that were too deep or otherwise unsuitable for lighthouse construction. To help mariners, the government placed these vessels, with lighthouse towers on board, in a location where there was a reef or hidden rocks.

My father bought a lightship that was considered surplus by the government. It was called the *Sambro Lightship* or Lightship #15. For over 50 years, this lightship had been a faithful guide at the entrance to Halifax harbour, greeting sailors from all around the world.

In dangerous, hurricane-force winds, the *Sambro Lightship* stayed her post, while others ran for safety. On the foggiest of nights, ships often came close to hitting her. She sat on guard during World War I and World War II, giving guidance and information to all during a time when there was no Global Positioning System (GPS) or even, in many cases, radar. I feel she deserves more notice. With today's modern navigation aids, some may find the lightships quaint, but they saved lives and ships.

In my research, I found a remark from a German U-boat captain. He said that they didn't want to sink the *Sambro Lightship* because "she kept the porch light on for us." Another story claimed that a U-boat commander used her as protection. He dove under her to escape charges.

When it was in operation, the lightship was manned by a crew of about 11 men. These men told stories of convoy ships being blown up by U-boat torpedoes and sinking within sight of the floating lighthouse. They reported that the blast was so powerful that it shook everything around them. The lightship was known to roll so much that even veteran sailors got seasick.

Eventually, she was replaced by a moor buoy, a fixed light, and sound device. Her removal was blamed for the *Cape Bonnie* going aground in 1967. The steel trawler belonging to National Sea Products Limited of Halifax hit a reef off Woody Island, Lower Prospect, just outside Halifax, on February 21, 1967. Eighteen men were lost at sea.

Tales From the Buccaneer Lodge

After my father bought the lightship, he brought her to the Dartmouth pier and placed one of my relatives aboard to serve as a watchman. Richard, an old sailor and a cousin of my grandmother's, came from Lunenburg. He loved his job. He fried up dory plug for anyone who came to visit him. My friends and I thought these greasy pieces of baloney were a delicacy.

I remember going aboard the lightship. The strong smell of oil, the enormous pistons in the engine room, and the ship's wooden ladders made it feel like a ghostly maze below deck. You could almost feel the presence of the men who lived on her in isolation from the rest of the world. Her living quarters were something like you would imagine on the *Titanic*. She was all mahogany. The beautiful woodwork, especially in the salon in the back of the ship, was something to be admired.

The lightship was expensive to keep. We had protected her from wild storms and vandalism; my father and his business partner wanted to get the best dollar for her, so they sold her while she was still in good shape. If I remember correctly, the buyer sailed her up the St. Lawrence River.

Frank Leaman

I think about her every time I look at a reproduction of a beautiful painting called "Sambro Lightship Guides Bluenose out of the Halifax harbour" by famed Nova Scotian artist Joseph Purcell. Like countless other Maritimers and people who love lighthouses and lightships, I am delighted she existed and I am proud of her work.

Averting a Second Halifax Explosion

The Halifax Explosion of 1917 is well known, but what happened to the Norwegian vessel SS *Trongate* is less well known. I would like to tell you what my father told me about the sinking of the *Trongate* in 1942 and a disaster that was averted.

The crew of the *Trongate* were known locally as a rough outfit. They drank a lot, played cards, and got in fights. For several months they had been stuck in port, with one delay after another. At one point, the *Trongate* was tied up in Dartmouth, waiting. She was loaded with ammunition, like TNT. She was very dangerous.

Tales From the Buccaneer Lodge

One night she sent out a shocking signal that she required immediate assistance because of a fire below deck. A ship filled with ammunition on fire in the Halifax harbour was a real threat to Canada and its war efforts. When the crew announced that they couldn't control the fire and were abandoning ship, and that fire boats were unable to contain the fire, the warship *Chedabucto* was called in to scuttle her.

The *Chedabucto* was given the job of sinking the 7,000-tonne *Trongate* by gunfire. As my father said, this was easier said than done—one wrong shell could bring disaster for all if she exploded. It was dangerous and risky. The *Chedabucto*'s crew did a great job of gunnery, hitting *Trongate* with practice shells filled with sand instead of ammunition along the waterline so that she would fill with water. *Trongate* drifted to what is called Dartmouth Cove. To remind me of what an explosion on board an ammunition ship can do, I often look at a twisted small cannon from the French munitions ship *Mont-Blanc*. When that ship exploded in Halifax harbour in 1917, the cannon landed in what

Frank Leaman

is now known as Mont-Blanc Cannon Park, located on the corner of Albro Lake Road and Pinecrest Drive in Dartmouth.

For about 45 minutes, the *Chedabucto* fired shells into the *Trongate*'s hull. She sank deeper into the water until finally she turned slightly on her side and disappeared. Left on the seabed of the harbour is a feature known as the "*Trongate* depression." Formed by the sinking of the vessel, it is a depression 125 metres in length, deeper at one end, with berms of mud. The largest berm extends 2 metres above the surrounding seabed, according to Natural Resources Canada.

When the ship went down, the city was saved from disaster and able to fight on in the war. If the situation had gone the other way and an explosion had taken place, would it have changed the course of the war? Certainly, my father's water transport company, among many others, probably would have gone up with the *Trongate*.

I often wonder what my father was thinking while the *Trongate* was burning in Halifax harbour. How did he and all the other men and women at the time deal with

Tales From the Buccaneer Lodge

serious threats like that and come out victorious? Don't they show us the way?

The *City of New York*

One day my father and I were driving down by the LaHave River, which winds its way through the South Shore from Annapolis County to the ocean. When we set out that day, I didn't know my father was looking for Captain Lou Kenedy, the infamous sailor known as the last schooner man.

From the 1920s until the 1980s, Captain Kenedy mastered ships delivering cargo up and down the eastern seaboard of North America from Nova Scotia to the Caribbean. Over this period, he is said to have skippered 10 vessels. There's even a book about his incredible life.

When my father spotted Captain Kenedy's sailboat tied up in the community of LaHave, he told me who I was about to meet. I was only a teenager, about 15 years old, and he was trying to make me understand what an impressive character Captain Kenedy was. We went aboard his beautiful sailing boat, which I think was named the *Sea Fox*. I was amazed that there was a fireplace aboard. My eyes were as big as sand dollars. One of the first things Captain Kenedy showed me was a trap door under which you could hide bottles of booze from the authorities, if you needed to.

Captain Kenedy didn't disappoint. Known as a solid, no-nonsense sailor, he and my father would talk about everything from the tropics to U-boats to all the larger-than-life characters he had met on his travels. Their conversations made a young man like me outward bound. I became lost in dreams of adventure, the romance of the sea sweeping me away. Amidst the smell of manila tarred rope, canvas, greased cable and chain, I had visions of billowing sails on the wide-open sea.

My father and Captain Kenedy did a lot of business together. Captain Kenedy used to haul lumber, including some from our mill, from Nova Scotia to New England on a storied ship called the *City of New York*. The schooner barque is best known for being Captain Richard E. Byrd's flagship on his exploration of Antarctica in the late 1920s, and more famously for possibly being the ship that didn't go to the aid of the *Titanic* in 1912.

After visiting Captain Kenedy, we went down to the wharf in Bridgewater, where his big old schooner lay. The LaHave River was dead calm. A wheezy old three-ton REO truck came down the wharf struggling to pick up the load of freshly sawn planks of mostly spruce wood from our mill. "Mad Man" was the name on the long hood of the two-door red truck. I knew its crew did not need the truck's name.

The *City of New York* looked tired, but she willingly accepted our lumber. All these years later, I can still remember the good, clean smell of just-sawn timber. It was heady to a lumberman. We had just bought some land near the LaHave River and it had given us a great harvest of large planks, or deals, as the old-timers called them.

Another heavily laden truck moved to the wharf to unload. The rattle of chains echoed across the wharf, along with the loud barking of orders. Everything appeared to be in order. To visit that lovely old schooner just hypnotized me.

Frank Leaman

I grew up around sailors and the sea, oblivious to the effects they were having on me. I looked up to men like Rear Admiral Richard Evelyn Byrd Jr., the American naval officer and explorer who received the highest honour for valour given by the United States. It was Rear Admiral Byrd who said, "Few men during their lifetime come anywhere near exhausting the resources dwelling within them. There are deep wells of strength that are never used."

Quotations from great men like Rear Admiral Byrd made me see a bigger world. Today, you can go to a museum and stare at rockets that took the first men into space, but when I was growing up, I learned about the explorers who made sea voyages to our planet's North and South poles. Songs that still exist today about the Northwest Passage, Franklin's lost expedition, and even Captain Kenedy called me to adventure, even if only in my dreams.

When I heard Neil Young's song "Captain Kennedy" later in my life, I thought more about the man I had met with my father in LaHave. I dug deeper into the *City of*

New York's life on the sea. She had a storied past. She had not only been the flagship of Rear Admiral Byrd on his exploration of Antarctica in the last 1920s but she had also been known before as the *Samson* and was possibly the ship that failed to help the *Titanic* in 1912.

In a deathbed statement, Henrik Bergethon Næss, the first officer on the *Samson* in 1912, claimed that on the night of April 14, 1912, he saw mast lights and distress signals on the horizon in the vicinity of the *Titanic*'s sinking. The *Samson* had no wireless equipment and thousands of illegal, frozen seal carcasses hunted from Canadian waters in her hold, according to his story. Fearing that the Coast Guard or the Royal Navy would hunt them down, she disappeared without helping the doomed *Titanic* passengers, most of whom lost their lives that night. Apparently, the people on board the *Samson* believed that the rockets desperately fired by *Titanic*'s crew were instead a Coast Guard cutter ready to arrest them. Other witnesses and evidence have cast doubt on Næss's statement. The mystery surrounding the *Titanic* and the *Samson* may never be solved.

City of New York.

To learn more of the *City of New York*'s story, visit the Yarmouth County Museum and Archives. They have what is left: artefacts and a nameplate from the bow of the ship. On one side of the plate is the name *Samson* and *City of New York* is on the other. The ship met her end not far from Yarmouth in 1952.

Captain Kenedy made his last trip on her that same year when he carried lumber from Sheet Harbour, Nova Scotia, to Quincy, near Boston. He sailed her back to Lunenburg and sold her to Quincy Lumber Company of Massachusetts. The plan was to use her to transport coal and potatoes between Massachusetts and Prince Edward

Island, but she needed repairs. On December 29, 1952, while she was being towed out of Yarmouth, the cable snapped. She was anchored, waiting to be moved again, when the tide dropped significantly, and she was grounded on a ledge. A stove in the cabin fell over, and fire broke out. The fire spread quickly, destroying most of her.

When I walked the decks of old schooners like *City of New York*, I pictured them as they might have been during their explorations in the North, when they were loaded with dozens of dogs and reindeer and equipment. Imagining their decks jammed with men and animals and supplies, these ships seemed very small. These ships and the men who sailed them put their lives in harm's way to help others and gain further knowledge that could help everyone. If it wasn't bad storms or ice they were dealing with, it was the threat of starvation or dog fights. One captain said that on his ship as many as 25 dog fights could break out in a day. These times have passed. Like shadows cast on a sundial, we pass too.

The Early Days of Cable Television in Rural Nova Scotia

A man I consider a great Canadian awarded me the cable television licence for Lunenburg, Bridgewater, and Mahone Bay. Pierre Juneau was the first chairman of the Canadian Radio-Television and Telecommunications Commission and was later president of the Canadian Broadcasting Corporation. The Juno Awards for Canadian musicians are named after him. He did so much to keep Canadian content alive in radio and television—he did his all to keep Canadian culture from being swamped by Americans.

For four days I sat in front of Juneau in 1975 while he questioned me about what I was going to do with the licence and how I would ensure that Canadian content was available for viewers. I am honoured that it was a man like Juneau who awarded the licence to me and my business partners, Dr. David Keddy and his brother Dr. Bruce Keddy, a surgeon at the Fishermen's Memorial Hospital in Lunenburg, and Barry Rofihe, a wealthy businessman from Bridgewater. We had stiff competition, but we got the licence.

The world of cable television wasn't completely new to me. In the late 1960s and early 1970s, my father started the Dartmouth cable station, one of Nova Scotia's first cable companies, with Charles Keating, a well-known businessman and philanthropist, and Garnet Brown, another successful local businessman and politician. About seven years later, my father sold his shares to Charles, who went on to successfully grow Dartmouth Cable and a cable empire.

Guests at the Buccaneer Lodge and aboard the *Buccaneer Lady* always brought us business ideas. Once on a charter-boat party, one of the guests showed me a quartz watch. I had never seen one before. The world's first quartz watch was unveiled by Seiko as the *Astron* in 1969. It was a big deal. The salesman told me that the quartz watch would revolutionize the watch industry, and he was right. A quartz watch or clock works by using an electronic oscillator that is regulated by a quartz crystal to keep time. The crystal oscillator creates a signal with precise frequency.

Our guests taught me more than once to believe in the quote by Thomas S. Monson, a former president of the Mormon Church: "We can't direct the wind, but we can adjust the sails."

We thanked our guests at the Buccaneer Resort for having introduced the idea of cable television to our family. Having operated a tourist business for so long, we hosted countless business meetings, church groups, and weddings where we met interesting people and listened to their ideas for how to make a quick buck or start a new successful business. When Garnet suggested that my father investigate cable television, he paid attention.

Cable television, a technique for transmitting information to and from a home, had been in Canada since 1952, but the industry experienced rapid growth in the decade between 1965 and 1975. In 1964, only 215,000

Frank Leaman

homes or 4 per cent of Canadian households subscribed to cable, according to the *Canadian Encyclopedia*. But a decade later, almost 60 per cent of Canadian households had it, and systems were in place to support its growth.

Garnet was a successful business leader and my father respected his opinion. In the mid-1950s, Garnet founded the brokerage firm A.G. Brown and Son Limited with his father and was one of the founders of Halifax Cablevision. He suggested that my father try for the cable licence for Dartmouth. He and my father were friends and he knew that my father was well known in the area and had come up the hard way to make a decent living for himself. He also knew that you needed a considerable amount of financial backing in order to get a loan from the bank, so he put my father in touch with Charles Keating.

Talk of cable TV and fibre optic cable was riveting and absorbing. It was the late 1960s and we wondered what in the devil fibre optics were. We knew we needed to learn more. We also started taking a real interest in what local programming existed in Halifax and thinking about how to prepare technically for a station. We took trips to Montreal and Toronto to see their cable systems.

We were so naive about it all, so we headed south to Washington to a huge cable convention. There, our eyes were opened to a new world. The Americans showed us pay television. We couldn't comprehend how it worked! They told us that it meant bringing movies into people's homes. We didn't understand how in the hell we were going to do that in little Nova Scotia, but we listened and learned. Also known as subscription television or premium television, pay TV was the early days of subscription-based television services.

The Americans also showed us fibre optic cable and told us that it would allow us to bring in 400 TV channels. When the Americans showed us all these things, we were blown away. They made it sound easy, but it proved to be anything but easy. The telephone companies wanted the cable television and made it difficult for us. Negotiating with them and the power companies to run our cable on their poles was sobering.

Changing people's habits and expectations was difficult

Frank Leaman

too. When my father got the Dartmouth licence and we told people we were going to charge them to watch their televisions, they laughed at us. It was a different time.

It took me and my business partners about two years to get a licence for Nova Scotia's South Shore and a $1 million loan from the Bank of Nova Scotia. When I got the open loan, interest on it was 7 per cent. When I got out of the business seven years later, interest on the loan had skyrocketed to 21 per cent. I got out by the skin of my teeth, but that was about all. Never in all my years in business had I ever experienced anything like the demands and restrictions of the local cable television industry.

In the mid-1970s, I started working at our cable station based in Blockhouse. We served the communities of Lunenburg, Bridgewater, Mahone Bay, and all the areas in between. Immediately I entered a competitive world with the CRTC demanding a serious commitment to local programming. Local programming was what Pierre Juneau wanted us to push, and we did. They were serious about it too. Representatives from the CRTC would periodically come down and check on me. They would

Tales From the Buccaneer Lodge

visit subscribers and ask whether I was doing a good job and how much local programming I was showing.

One of the conditions for my licence was that I had to bring in the CBC's French channel from Halifax. It wasn't easy. It was a poor signal from the city. On a stormy day the signal was even worse and would go wavy, leaving viewers with a poor-quality picture. My engineer and I worked hard to improve the signal, but we didn't have much luck.

One morning at the gas station in Bridgewater, the man operating the pumps asked me, "Frank, can't you get that French channel clearer?"

"Do you speak French?" I asked, surprised.

"No," said the man. "Haven't you seen those movies on late at night?"

I hadn't. He told me about the nudity in them and I quickly realized that they were a little more risqué than the family-friendly movies I was used to. *Vive la différence*, I thought.

I was a natural for running a local television station, having been curious and community minded since the time I was a young boy. I also understood Lunenburg

Frank Leaman

County. But there is a difference between understanding a community and wanting to help it and being able to respond adequately to its needs. When the station opened, a kaleidoscope opened to me and I had to respond. Talented local musicians, artists, craftspeople, farmers, politicians, school boards—they all wanted to have their say. I dove in, recognizing the need to help address local problems. I even began telethons to raise money for Bonny Lea Farm, a local organization helping people with intellectual disabilities.

My area was loaded with talent just waiting to be discovered. Thank goodness that so many wonderful people responded. Joyce Seamone came to see me. She was a Canadian country singer who was known for her 1972 hit "Testing 1 2 3." I put her on TV. I wasn't a big aficionado of country music, but I knew my audience was. I remember going to the Lunenburg Exhibition to hear country music. I wasn't really interested but I went to learn more about it and to tape the concert for my cable customers.

I knew some of the musicians who came to see me since I was a teenager. One of them was Bobby Curtola.

Tales From the Buccaneer Lodge

The Canadian rock and roll singer came to my rescue. He had many songs on the music charts: "Hand in Hand with You" in 1960, "Indian Giver," "Aladdin," and his biggest chart topper, "Fortune Teller," in 1962, which reportedly sold 2.5 million copies. Curtola had fallen in love with the South Shore and bought a home there. He played on television and supported us however he could. This was the start of something big for everyone.

When a committed group of civic-minded people in the Chester area started a local project that would become Bonny Lea Farm, I knew I had to help. I was motivated by Pierre Juneau's urges to support local programming and Canadian content and the example set by my doctor, Dr. S. Laufer. Dr. Laufer was not only a respected doctor but the benefactor of many institutions. He encouraged me.

After Bonny Lea Farm (the South Shore Community Service Association) was established on 80 acres of land in Chester in 1973, I held two telethons to raise money for them. Local musicians and entertainers came from all over the county. With help from Halifax, I got the shows on the road, and it was a success. The telethon attracted

Frank Leaman

more local talent and the creation of local programs on our cable channel.

What our audiences liked were shows they could interact with. "Coffee Time with Tom" was one of them. It was a call-in, shoot-your-mouth-off show. It always got a lot of callers. At the time, we weren't allowed to have advertising on our community channel. We figured out how to get around that: bring products onto the set. On a talk show host's table might be a beautiful bouquet of flowers from the local flower shop down the road.

Our audiences also loved what I called a live-in-the-sky show. To create that, we travelled around the local area, filmed beautiful places, and then aired the footage, with soft music playing in the background. It was simple, but people loved it.

We also had a lot of church groups on the station. They would come, play the guitar, sing, and give a sermon. One East Indian group spoke about Brahman, the Hindu god, and played instruments we didn't usually hear, like the sitar.

Outside of music and religion and talk shows, I also

covered local school board meetings. We would tape the meetings, which often got quite heated, and later air them. To promote the area, I visited tourist attractions. I might visit a mill and tell its history. I was honoured to have my work recognized; I received an award for my commitment to local programming at a cable TV convention in Toronto.

When we first got the cable licence for Dartmouth, there was no microwave in the area to import signals from the United States. We paid people to sit on one of the high peaks of Chamcook Mountain, near Saint Andrews, New Brunswick, with an antenna to trap American signals coming out of Bangor, Maine. They would tape the popular shows on VCR and bring the tapes to Dartmouth, where we would air them. We also sold the tapes to the station in Yarmouth.

The problem with that system was bad weather. It interfered with the signals, and when that happened, there was trouble. I remember coming home from work one day and my housekeeper turning to me and saying angrily, "Frank, you said that when we got this cable TV from the US we'd have all the shows we wanted." She explained that her beloved show wasn't on. "Richard isn't even out of prison yet," she went on.

"Who is Richard?" I asked.

I found out he was one of the main characters in the popular daytime soap opera *Days of Our Lives*. When the weather was unpredictable, the airing of the next episode of the soap opera could be delayed. Sometimes we broadcasted weather reports from Bangor that were a week old. We learned to start deleting those before we put a show on air.

If there was a problem in the transmission of the popular American miniseries *Rich Man, Poor Man*, I knew I needed to hide. Everyone wanted to watch it. Some mornings I had to sneak to the post office to avoid angry people.

Back then, people were serious about watching television. They were dedicated to their shows. On Saturday nights, Charlie Tenan came on wearing a cowboy hat, leather chaps, and boots, holding a piece of bristol board that read: *Frankenstein's Country Jamboree*. The show started in Maine in 1963 before switching to simply

Tales From the Buccaneer Lodge

the *Country Jamboree* in 1969. In 1973, Dick Stacey took over sole sponsorship, and the show became *Dick Stacey's Country Jamboree*. It remained a hit in Maine and the Maritimes for years, until it ended its regular run in 1984. A generation of local country music fans grew up on that show, which hosted amateur musicians from the whole region. They'd say things like, "Herbert, come up now and sing your song." And Herbert would come up from the audience and sing a song, accompanied by guitar. It was very authentic, and viewers loved the show.

They always played the song "Wings of a Dove." We couldn't believe that this simple show coming out of Maine was a hit, but it was. Stacey was a funny-looking, bald man. He'd shove his hands up to the TV screen and say, "See these hands? They pump gas! And they stink!" I think he owned several gas stations. And then he'd say, "We'll pump gas for you, so your hands don't stink."

For all this and more, my customers paid me $7.50 per month to subscribe to the station. We needed every cent of it. I had almost enough subscribers to really make it work. But I was nervous the whole time that the bank would call in our loans. I could see interest rates rising and some of my business partners were having personal problems. I knew I had to find a buyer. Luckily, I found one: John Bragg.

Known as the wild blueberry king, as well as a giant processor of carrots and other food commodities, in 1968 he founded Oxford Frozen Foods in 1968 in Oxford, Nova Scotia. A few years later he founded what would become Bragg Communications. It was later expanded to become Eastlink, a communications company that is now a regional force in the Maritimes.

Bragg bought me out in the late 1970s. By that time, I was paying 21 per cent on a $1 million loan and struggling to stay afloat. I thanked God for the blueberry king.

Surplus Goods

One Man's Waste ...

My father had a knack for buying cheap surplus goods from the war. He instinctively knew how to turn one man's waste into another man's treasure.

At the beginning of World War II, my father scoured the province for a boat. Because his eyesight was bad, the Canadian Army had turned him down. He knew he had to help the war efforts in some other way. Having spent his whole life living off the harbour—selling lobsters and anything else he could fish from the water—he thought he could best help with a boat.

Boats of any type were hard to get at the time, but

Frank Leaman

somewhere around Peggy's Cove, he found the *Audrey Kaye*; he paid a substantial price for her. She was a fishing boat, just under 50 feet long, with a gas engine. Gasoline was rationed during the war. Somehow he got the fuel he needed to keep that boat running non-stop. The *Audrey Kaye* did valuable duty during the war hauling seamen, military personnel, freight, and whatever else was necessary. My father's *Audrey Kaye* didn't look pretty, but she proved strong. With his efforts and those of his crew, they helped the country's at-home service.

Just after he married my mother, Helen, my father took her down to the harbour to proudly show her what he had purchased with their money. In the back of the boat was a pile of dirty-looking rope. My father was proud of it; my mother almost cried. "You spent our money on that?" was all she could say.

"You don't understand. The finest paper was made of that rope," he told her, surprised she couldn't see the boat's potential.

My father often told me stories about wartime Halifax and his dangerous trips criss-crossing the harbour. One

Tales From the Buccaneer Lodge

of the *Audrey Kaye*'s main jobs was hauling sailors from Halifax up the Bedford Basin to the convoy ships. This was a job that happened at all hours of the day and night. During the war years, the harbour and waterfront were jammed with people and boats and noise. Dozens of vessels would gather in the basin, where they were loaded with troops, munitions, and supplies. These huge groups of ships, known as convoys, would sail back to Europe together, accompanied by armed naval escort vessels.

Before they left the harbour, the ships had to stop at an examining battery off McNab's Island at the mouth of the harbour. There, two small boats had to pull back a section of the anti-submarine net that was stretched across the harbour to allow them through. The net was always closed to prevent undetected enemy submarines from entering the harbour. This huge curtain of steel hoops that hung between the surface of the water and the bottom of the harbour was held in place by buoys.

Just outside the harbour's netted gate, German U-boats were busy blowing up anything they could.

Frank Leaman

Many times, the convoy sailors my father transported on the *Audrey Kaye* were victims of these attacks. Others suffered from nervous breakdowns. I was told of one incident in which a sailor jumped into the harbour and hid under the wharf instead of going aboard the *Audrey Kaye* with his fellow sailors. Forced to surface, the shore patrol grabbed him, put warm, dry clothes on him, and sent him back to the convoy.

After my father dropped the sailors to their convoy ships, he would ask them if they had anything to sell; often they had a bit of rope or paint to offer. He would scrounge enough money together to buy it and later resell it, making just enough to provide food and a warm place to live for me and my mother.

My father was out on the *Audrey Kaye* at all hours of the day and night and in all types of weather. He built a larger cabin on the boat to provide some protection from the elements. When he wasn't transporting people, it was supplies. All around the harbour there was activity. At HMC Dockyard and the busy facilities of the Halifax shipyard came the constant sound of hammers, saws, and the popping and crackling of welding torches repairing or refitting ships. There was endless repair work to be done on the ships. The damage was caused mostly by storms, collisions in a convoy, or from enemy action. Several small ship-repair shops helped with the work done at the shipyard. My father often transported supplies to and from these places.

The fact that we later did many cruises, tours, and tuna-fishing trips at the Buccaneer Lodge had its genesis in Halifax harbour when my father ran harbour transit during the war years. His harbour duty, with its smell of manila rope, tar, bunker oil, and the sound of large engines throbbing, was a world away from Chester and Mahone Bay, where duty was sunny days, cawing seagulls, and guitar music. But a price must be paid if you want to work anywhere with boats and serve the public. As the American author John Shedd wrote, "A ship in harbour is safe, but that is not what ships are built for."

Frank Leaman

VE Day Riots

I was at the VE day riots that broke out at the end of the war in Halifax and Dartmouth, but I was too young to remember anything. That must have been the thing to do—take your child to the riots. Yes, I was pushed by my parents in my baby carriage sitting atop several bottles of booze.

The history books explain it this way: on May 7 and 8, 1945, riots broke out after Victory in Europe celebrations fell apart in the city. Several thousand servicemen, mostly those from the Navy, merchant seamen, and civilians drank, then vandalized and looted. My parents got some of this booze, which they then stashed in my baby carriage. At the time, restaurants and hotels in Halifax were not allowed to sell liquor. Private clubs could, but servicemen were not permitted to join. The only place to buy alcohol was from government stores. Other than the wet messes on the bases, illegal clubs and brothels were the only places where sailors could drink.

According to the story my parents told me, the liquor store by the railroad station just south of the Angus L.

Tales From the Buccaneer Lodge

Macdonald Bridge in Dartmouth was closed. There weren't enough police officers around to patrol everything. A crowd broke into the store to get their hooch. While sailors danced with stolen mannequins on Barrington Street and cavorted in the Grand Parade, the rest of the city celebrated the war's end however they could.

Tensions were high. People had been living with the Nazis at our harbour gates and had seen ships with gigantic holes blown in their sides in the shipyards and service people from everywhere packing the streets. It was said that there were as many as 25,000 servicemen in Halifax during the war and this was straining the city's limited resources.

Atlantic Kon-Tiki

When several Frenchmen showed up at the Dartmouth Marine Slips in 1956 looking for Douglas fir poles to build a raft to cross the ocean, they called my father. For some time, our company, Dartmouth Woodworkers, was one of the main suppliers of the wood slips used to repair wooden ships. The Dartmouth Marine Slips are no longer, but between the mid-1850s and 2003 it was an important shipyard and marine railway. It was especially important during the Battle of the Atlantic in World War II. After it closed, a wealthy developer bought the site and built fancy high-rise condominiums on the property and called it King's Wharf.

We had the poles the Frenchmen wanted. My father had salvaged them from HMCS Albro Lake, a naval radio station operated by the Royal Canadian Navy. The poles were surplus from when radio masts had been installed at the station. Established in 1942, the station was several kilometres north of Dartmouth.

Henri Beaudout, a young Frenchman who moved to Canada after World War II, had the idea to build a raft and set sail. He had heard of a similar voyage across the Pacific. In 1947, Thor Heyerdahl sailed a log raft called *Kon-Tiki* from Peru to the Polynesian islands. Henri wanted to be the first to cross the Atlantic on a raft.

In 1956, Henri convinced a few of his friends to join

him. The men arrived in Halifax with the idea of building the raft out of telephone poles. But as the story goes, the phone poles they originally found from the telephone company were made of white cedar. They didn't want them. Eventually they found my father.

The Frenchmen didn't speak much English, but my father was able to communicate to them that we had the logs they wanted. Intrigued by their ambitious project, and maybe a little guilty to be aiding them, my father wouldn't take money from the men. I think his conscience wouldn't allow it, considering the strong possibility they might drown in the middle of the Atlantic Ocean.

At the Dartmouth shipyard, it took months to build their raft with its small hut on top. They called it *L'Egare II* (*The Lost One 2*). Henri had launched his first raft the year before from Montreal. It met its end off the coast of Newfoundland.

Everyone the men met told them not to make the voyage—including the Canadian Coast Guard—but despite the warnings they left Dartmouth in May 1956. They took two kittens with them. The shipyard had a lot of

Frank Leaman

feral cats at the time. The Frenchmen decided the kittens would keep them company on the long voyage.

When a woman got wind of their plan, she got upset. She called the Nova Scotia SPCA to investigate. Someone from the animal protection agency came and told the Frenchmen bluntly, "You guys can die, but the kittens can't." The animals were taken off the raft. But the day they pushed away from the wharf, the cats were back on board.

When they reached the Grand Banks of Newfoundland, fishermen were surprised to see the men floating around on big poles, tied tightly together with rope. One crew member got sick, was maybe even starting to go a little crazy, and had to be rescued. The remaining three crew and two kittens made it safely to Britain surviving on rations, fishing, and drinking cans of water.

The kittens were adopted by a member of the Royal Family who had heard about their adventurous tale. They were said to be treated like royalty for the rest of their lives. Sadly, the same didn't happen for the raft's crew. *L'Egare II* was soon forgotten. More than 50 years later that began to change when two Canadian journalists helped revive the story and eventually turn it into an award-winning documentary. In 2017, author Ryan Barnett and illustrator Dmitry Bondarenko told the story in their book *The Raftsmen*.

In 2016, 60 years after they had set sail from what is now King's Wharf, a plaque celebrating their ocean-going feat was unveiled at the spot. Henri, the last surviving member of the crew, was there to mark the occasion. I was also there.

"Every time I talked about it, everybody thought I was crazy," Henri told CBC News reporter Carolyn Ray through a translator at the Dartmouth event. "It was the first time that anybody did this in the world. But it didn't make us supermen."

The *Candy Apple*

Our job at the Buccaneer was to be ready to warmly receive travellers—whenever and from wherever they came. We usually pulled off this feat with the countless

Frank Leaman

The *Candy Apple*.

Tales From the Buccaneer Lodge

visitors who arrived at our door after journeying aboard fancy yachts or more modest boats. But when a concrete-hulled schooner, stretching about 85-feet long arrived, we weren't able to help them the way we would have liked.

The story its crew told us started in Toronto in the mid-1970s. Built out of a reported 52 tons of concrete by a Toronto couple, the boat was painted bright red and called the *Candy Apple*. Before setting off down the St. Lawrence River on its way to the East Coast, it had been moored at the foot of Leslie Street in Toronto and was home to Nevin and Carol Coleman, their four-year-old son, and their dog, Sailor. The family's plan was to set sail on a three-year trip around the world. To help share the cost of their dream voyage, they asked some compatible people to join them. They all planned to sail around the world together on a concrete ship adventure. Everything on the boat's exterior looked good, but problems soon started to arise.

After a happy send-off in Toronto that attracted quite a crowd, they discovered a leak, which caused the boat to take on water. Despite the leak, they made it as far as

Frank Leaman

Summerside, Prince Edward Island. Some of the boat's investors started getting nervous and jumped ship, so to speak. We had a captain friend in Summerside who put them in touch with us. He told them we could find the right boat builder to fix their boat.

When they arrived at the Buccaneer, we tried to help, but soon the reality of their situation became clear. Experienced boat carpenters at the shipyard in Dartmouth told them that she wouldn't survive an ocean crossing. While the owners decided what to do next, she rested, tied up at the public wharf in Chester. It was there in the front harbour that she met her end. Caught in a terrible storm, she turned on her side and partially sank. With her port side sticking out of the water, she was now in worse trouble and a menace to other boats. She stayed for a time in limbo and became derelict. In a decision that probably saved several lives, she was towed out to sea and sunk.

Having owned several boats, I discovered the hard way that you must be prepared to pay the price. As one old sailor I knew used to say, "it's not the hull that costs, it's the riggings." But in the case of the *Candy Apple*, it proved to be the other way around. Boats aren't meant to be made of concrete.

Little Brooklyn Ball Park

My father and I worked a lot; we had no other choice. But our lives weren't all work. We found some time to have fun. My father loved parties, going to them and throwing them whether at the Buccaneer Lodge or at his house in Dartmouth. One of his frequent guests was Garnet Brown, a well-known Dartmouth businessman and later provincial politician. Brown served as a Member of the Legislative Assembly in the Halifax-Eastern Shore riding from 1969 to 1978. During that time, he also served as Minister of Highways and Public Works and Minister of Tourism. Born in 1930, he was an athletic boy and a heck of a baseball player. He was signed by the Brooklyn Dodgers and played on its farm team for a couple of years.

Frank Leaman

When Garnet came by my father's house, he never came alone. He'd bring baseball players from the Dartmouth Arrows team. They were champions of the Halifax and District Baseball League. They used to train and play at the ballpark, located about five blocks from our mill on the Dartmouth waterfront, at the base of the Angus L. Macdonald Bridge.

Inside the park was a large stadium with floodlights that would light up the field on long summer nights. It was a popular spot in the 1950s. It doesn't exist anymore. In

Tales From the Buccaneer Lodge

its place today is the Holiday Inn Harbourview hotel. In its heyday, they used to say the stadium took up to 7,000 people, but I think the crowds were more like 5,000. It was a popular spot. Kids who had no money used to sneak in through the boards in the stands to watch the exciting games. A Catholic church in Dartmouth used to sell programs for the games. I seem to remember them being 15 cents a copy. You could also buy tickets for a prize of $25, a good bit of money at the time.

I liked to watch the games, but I liked it even more when Garnet would bring the players and umpire Johnny Fortunato to my father's house for a few drinks. They loved to gather in the basement and sit on the barstools lined up along the long bar that he had made of shellacked knotty pine boards. They'd sit there for hours, smoking and drinking. They had seen the Humphrey Bogart movies and did a pretty good job imitating them.

Frank Leaman

Mic Mac Amateur Aquatic Club

On the shores of Lake Banook in downtown Dartmouth stands the Mic Mac Amateur Aquatic Club, now a busy paddling and rowing spot. I used to go there on summer nights when I was a young fella of 16 or 17. The club first opened in 1923, long before there was even a small boat house. In the early days, the club's emphasis was on social events. The club's commitment to paddling and rowing grew and, in 1932, it sent four men to the Los Angeles Olympic Games to compete for Canada in the men's four rowing event.

When a clubhouse was built, it was exiting to go to the dances inside. It was just like the movies depicting the perfect summer romance. Those warm nights were like a dream. We had fun listening to Kenny Weeks and the Meteors playing "Red Sails to the Sunset," Bill Haley's "Rock around the Clock," and Little Richard's "Tutti Fruiti." Kenny Weeks had been the opening act for the American rock and roll band Bill Haley and His Comets. He had a great stunt where he would pretend to

Tales From the Buccaneer Lodge

be Jerry Lee Lewis and pound the keys of his keyboard with his heel. I'd never seen anything like it in real life. The dance hall was upstairs at the club. On a still night, you could go out on the balcony and look out over the lake as the music and merriment from the hall softly rang out across the water.

Moving On

Selling the Buccaneer

I finally talked my father into selling the Buccaneer in the late 1970s. We had to get rid of it; we couldn't afford to own it anymore. We were actually paying money to keep it going. It was still busy, but it couldn't carry itself. My father was spending too much. He and his friends led a lavish lifestyle and it was costing us.

To me it felt like we were running a candy store filled with all the wonderful treats sugar-loving children dream of buying for pennies. But if this candy store cost us $1,000 a day to run, we were only making $800 in sales every day. It was the same problem at the Buccaneer:

we weren't bringing in enough money. We were happy when we found a buyer who decided to stop running the Buccaneer as a lodge. He eventually sold shares and transformed the business into vacation properties.

After the sale, I still had several businesses to run, including the cable company for the South Shore. By 1990, I was tired from my decades as a hardscrabble entrepreneur. I wanted to work for someone else and have them—not me—worry about the tax bill, the light bill, the heat bill, and employees' pay cheques. I went to work for Sears department store at Penhorn Mall, just down the road from my house in Dartmouth. I wasn't sure how I was going to handle not being the boss, but I stayed there until 1997.

My new job in sales in the store's lawn and garden department felt like a vacation, like I was a stranger in a new land. My years of dealing with customers, particularly at the Buccaneer Lodge, served me well. Understanding management was sometimes more difficult. I found out the hard way that I had to do things their way.

After a shipment of lawn mower accessories arrived,

Tales From the Buccaneer Lodge

I went to work putting the products on shelves. My floor manager almost threw a fit when he saw me in action. "No, no, no! It isn't placed right. It must be placed according to the plan," he told me, as he pulled out what looked like a book. Inside, there was a detailed map that showed the exact location of every product and item.

I realized that I had been hired to follow orders. Sometimes this wasn't so easy, because the orders weren't clear. Sears was a well-respected, full-service, national retail chain at the time. It prided itself on training its employees and offering its customers top service. It also boasted a money-back guarantee. Management explained to us more specifically that this was a "money-back guarantee unless ..." *Unless* was the key word. I was supposed to be like a fortune teller who could look into the future and make the right decision as to when "unless" applied.

In the lawn and garden department, I was told I should take back mowers unless they looked as though they had been used commercially. It took a couple of times before I caught on to what this really meant. The first time I dealt with a customer dissatisfied with a product was when an

Frank Leaman

elderly lady came in with her weed whacker that looked more like weed kill than a machine that could trim grass and weeds. I looked at it and said that I would not be able to take it back because of its poor condition. She got visibly angry and said she would not leave the store until I reversed my decision. In the middle of the department, in front of everyone, she sat down on the floor, and waited. Before long, the floor manager of my department arrived on the scene and instructed me to give the lady a new weed whacker, no questions asked.

Another time a customer came in with an electric lawn mower that was so worn I thought it had to have been used commercially. He wanted me to take it back and give him a new one. I refused, and he complained to management. I came back to work the next day and there was a new electric lawn mower with a tag attached to it. On the tag was the customer's name. My manager explained to me that the customer was a good customer who bought many products and therefore had to be kept happy.

I soon realized that our job was to minimize embarrassing scenes. Embarrassing scenes are not good

Tales From the Buccaneer Lodge

for business. Our job was to make customers happy and give them the best service possible. We received a lot of training on products and even paid home visits if a customer had difficulty figuring out how to use their new mower. I once saw a colleague arguing with a customer. After the customer left, my colleague was escorted out of the building and I never worked with him again.

Providing top-quality service provided difficult for Sears Canada to maintain as the market changed. Across the country, the department-store chain began feeling the pressures of increased competition from American retail giants. When a Walmart store moved in next door to Sears, I was confronted daily with customers complaining that they could get a product cheaper there. My years of fighting in the arena of the small business world made me realize how lucky I was to let Sears handle those challenging times.

I never knew who I was going to serve during a shift at Sears. One day before the holidays, I was busy decorating a large, artificial Christmas tree when two rough-looking men approached me and said they wanted to buy the tree.

Frank Leaman

It was for a politician who had once been well known in the province, they told me. The tree, with all its ornaments, cost about $500, a considerable sum at the time. I wondered why these men wanted it for the politician.

"Where is he?" I asked them.

"Here," they said, and pointed to an old, rundown wheelchair. Looking small and hidden in the chair next to the big, gruff men sat a man I immediately recognized, not only as a prominent political figure but someone I used to serve at the Buccaneer Lodge. He no longer looked like the powerful politician he once was, but instead he looked weakened by Alzheimer's disease or some other form of dementia. Looking at him, I was reminded of the saying, "History never really says goodbye. History says, 'See you later.'" I remember the old politician looking at me that day in the store and smiling.

In 1997, it was time for me to retire from Sears. I had developed edema, a swelling in my feet, ankles, and legs, and my doctor ordered me to spend less time standing. Sears struggled in the subsequent years, but it would be another 20 years before the store in Penhorn Mall closed for good.

I've often wondered why I always gravitated to boats and the water. You could say it's in my genes. All you need to do is look back at the lives of my father and grandfather. Not everyone has a grandfather who in 1936 built his own 23-foot wooden sailboat and then set sail from Halifax harbour, bound for Vancouver on a solo, 14-month journey that took him through the Panama Canal.

I always got an unforgettable feeling when I was out on the water. I felt like I was free. Truly free. My feeling of freedom wasn't unique. Humphrey Bogart was fond of saying, "I think Hemingway said one time that the sea is the last free place on earth." The world has changed dramatically in the decades since then, but maybe that sense of the sea as a place of freedom hasn't changed.

If my memory serves me correctly, it was 1961 when we left Chester aboard the *Buccaneer Lady* en route to Cape Breton Island. A group of American boaters had made the trip up from Marblehead, Massachusetts, and were headed to Baddeck, a town on the northern shore of Bras d'Or Lake. With my father at the helm, we travelled in convoy with a few boats. As we got further up the rocky coast, we lost sight of the other boats. All we had were ourselves and the ocean. It felt good. Instead of feeling fear, I felt freedom. At that moment, everything was right with the world. It wasn't really, but I felt it was because we were on the water.

I rarely get that feeling anymore. I'm an old man now. I've managed to live longer than my father, who died in 1993. He was only 72 years old. It's harder for me to get around now so I stay close to shore, but my memories haven't left me—they're still very much alive, deep within me.

Frank Leaman

ABOUT THE AUTHOR

Born in Dartmouth, Nova Scotia in 1942, Frank Leaman spent most of his life living and working in his hometown on the eastern shore of Halifax harbour.

After studying business for one year at a vocational school in Halifax, Frank helped his father, Frank Manual Leaman, run the family's seven businesses, including a sawmill and a local cable company.

Frank has five children, nine grandchildren and one great-grandchild. He still lives in Dartmouth where he writes and is a member of the Evergreen Writers Group. Frank's previous book, *The Roar of the Sea*, also published by Boulder Books, is a fascinating recollection of the dramatic sailing adventures of his grandfather, Captain William A. Crowell.

Buccaneer Resort Lodge.